Blame It
on the
Butterflies

R.A. McGraw

Blame It on the Butterflies

© 2025 Ryan McGraw

All rights reserved.

This is a work of fiction. Names, characters, places, and incidents are either products of the author's imagination or used fictitiously. Any resemblance to actual persons, living or dead, or real events is purely coincidental.

For permissions, inquiries, or rights requests, contact:
BlameitontheButterflies@gmail.com

First Edition: 2025

ISBN: 979-8-9987599-0-1

Cover design by Bojan R @pixelstudio

Printed in the United States of America

Acknowledgments

This book was written with love, grief, and the belief that stories can heal what silence cannot.

To my family and friends—thank you for standing by me, for giving me space to grow, and for reminding me of who I am when I forget. Your love shaped these pages more than you know.

To every teacher, mentor, and artist who ever told me I had something worth sharing—thank you for planting that seed. This is the bloom.

To those who live with pain but still find ways to love: this story is for you.

To Uzi—for the light you represent, and to every child who reminds us what it means to be kind.

To Brent—for the fathers who show up, and the ones who try, and the ones who carry more than they can name.

To A.V.—for turning pain into power.

To every reader who made it to the end: I hope something here stays with you. Not because it was perfect. But because it was true.

Lastly, to the butterflies—seen and unseen. You were always the story.

Dedication

For those who love hard, break soft, and keep going anyway.
For every child who ever felt too much.
And for the one who still believes in heroes.

Table of Contents

The Sound of
the Streets

Butterflies can remember being caterpillars. Scientists call
this "cellular memory." Even after total transformation, part
of them still knows where they began.

T he summer heat in his neighborhood didn't walk—it stalked.

It rolled down from rooftops and clung to shirt collars,
seeped into shoes, made the pavement sweat. But A.V. didn't care.
He was nine years old, shirt soaked through, hooping with his crew
in the middle of the street like the world belonged to them.

The ball bounced sharp—thwack-thwack—clap off the rusted rim
nailed to someone's garage. Malik was guarding too close, and Jairo
kept calling fouls that didn't exist, but none of that mattered. It was
summer. And it was theirs.

A boombox sat on the curb playing Nas one minute, DMX the next—
bass rattling like loose change in a soda can. Somebody's cousin had
rigged it up to a car battery, and it made the whole block hum.

"Yo, double or nothin'!" A.V. shouted, dribbling with one hand and holding his shorts up with the other. They were two sizes too big—his uncle's old pair. The drawstring was long gone.

"You owe me a soda already!" Malik hollered. "You not gettin' two!"

A.V. grinned, then drove left. The boys scattered, sneakers squeaking on pavement. He launched a shot with terrible form but raw confidence. It banked hard off the backboard—and in.

"Buckets!" he shouted, arms to the sky. "King me!"

"You think this chess, dummy?" Malik said, laughing, already chasing the ball.

That's when the shots rang out.

Three pops. Sharp, distant. From somewhere across the avenue, maybe behind the liquor store.

No one screamed. No one ran.

A.V. dropped to the ground automatically—so did the others. Like a drill they'd done a thousand times, heads low, bellies pressed to sun-scorched pavement. The boombox kept playing like nothing happened.

They waited five seconds. Then ten.

"Sounded far," Jairo muttered.

A.V. nodded and sat up. "Yeah. Wrong side of the street."

Nobody said anything more about it. Malik stood up and brushed gravel off his knees as the basketball bounced once, twice, then sailed over a rusted chain-link fence into someone's yard.

"You gettin' that?" he asked, smirking at A.V.

"Man, I hit the shot," A.V. said. "That's your punishment."

But he was already climbing.

The fence rattled under his shoes. He dropped down on the other side with a soft grunt—knees bent, palms catching dirt. The basketball sat beneath a bent lawn chair, half-deflated, looking just as tired as the neighborhood.

The house behind the chair loomed quiet—curtains drawn, paint peeling from the siding in wide, sunburnt strips. An empty stroller lay tipped on its side near the porch. Wind chimes clinked in the breeze, off-beat and out of tune.

A.V. picked up the ball and hesitated.

He could smell it—vinegar, weed smoke, burnt oil, hot plastic. The scent of a place that hadn't been cleaned in weeks but was still lived in. Still survived in.

"Let's go, man!" Malik shouted from the sidewalk. "You move slower than your Wi-Fi!"

Jairo cracked up behind him, that loud, loose laugh that always hit a second too late.

A.V. turned to climb back over the fence, but before he could, the screen door creaked open.

Mrs. Daniels.

She was ancient, with skin like wrinkled leather and one cloudy eye that never quite looked at you. But she was sharp. Mean, too, if she didn't like your energy.

A.V. froze.

"You boys playin' in the damn street again?" she growled.

"Yes, ma'am."

"You get down when them shots went off?"

"Yes, ma'am."

She sniffed. "Good. That means somebody taught you somethin'."

A breath.

"Was my boy out there?"

A.V. shifted. "Don't think so. Ain't seen him all day."

Mrs. Daniels nodded slowly.

"If he shows up, you tell him I'm not mad. Just want him home before sundown."
She hesitated.
"Been a couple days since I seen him."

"Yes, ma'am."

"Take that ball and go on. And tell that loud little boy to quit hollerin' like a fool—ain't nobody impressed with that lopsided fade."

"Yes, ma'am."

A.V. climbed the fence again, slower this time—thinking about Mrs. Daniels' son.

Kid was maybe sixteen. Ran with a crew out in Englewood. Used to be around all the time—laugh too loud, hands too soft for the life he was trying to live, eyes always carrying something he didn't talk about.

Like he'd seen something he shouldn't have, or missed something he couldn't get back.

A.V. remembered the last time he saw him—standing on the curb with his hoodie half-zipped and his fists clenched, like he was either about to cry or swing. Said he was "done with all that," but never said what *that* was.

Then he just stopped coming around.

And that usually meant one of three things:
Locked up. Laid low. Or laid out.

Nobody ever said which.

Back on the street, he tossed the ball to Malik and didn't say anything about the exchange.

They played for another twenty minutes before the sun burned the energy right out of them.

The court shimmered like glass, sneakers dragging more than they bounced. No one wanted to be the first to tap out—so they all just sort of drifted off, like it had been the plan all along.

Basketball under one arm, A.V. led the pack down the block.

It wasn't a long street, just loud. Life spilled from every corner.

On the left side, Mr. Terrence sat on an upturned milk crate with a chessboard balanced on a cardboard box. He played himself most days, whispering strategy out loud like he was teaching an invisible student.

"Queen takes knight. You ain't see that comin', huh?" he muttered, moving the piece with a crooked grin.

He spotted the boys and nodded. "Stay smart, little generals."

"Always," A.V. called back, giving a salute.

Farther down, a woman stood in a doorway braiding her daughter's hair, the girl squirming like a worm in the sun. The smell of grease and Blue Magic hung thick in the air.

"You keep moving, I'ma braid your scalp!" the mother snapped, fingers moving lightning fast.

The girl spotted A.V. and smiled. "Hi, Avery!"

He flashed a peace sign and kept walking, ears burning.

Behind them, music thumped from a cracked-open garage—someone spinning vinyl, probably DJ Ellis. It wasn't a party, not yet, but the vibe was getting there. Kids danced in driveways. Boys rode bikes in loops. A toddler in nothing but a diaper chased bubbles blown by his big sister.

The block wasn't perfect. But it was breathing.

The buildings leaned on each other like tired old men. Power lines sagged. Lawns were patchy, if they existed at all. But every porch had chairs on it. And someone to sit in them. Every stoop had a story, and every story mattered to someone.

A.V. slowed as they passed a corner store—graffiti-tagged but open, always open. A man outside leaned against the wall, smoking something stronger than cigarettes. Eyes red. Shirt hanging open. He didn't say anything. Didn't have to.

Jairo whispered, "That's your cousin?"

A.V. didn't answer. He just kept walking.

A.V. split from the crew at the corner, dapping them up without a word. Malik tossed the ball high and caught it behind his back like a magician, hollering something stupid as he turned the other way.

A.V. didn't laugh. Didn't even smile.

The closer he got to his house, the quieter he got inside. Like he was folding himself up, piece by piece. Voice, gone. Shoulders, lower. Eyes, sharp but small.

The paint on the front door had chipped away in layers, like it was trying to forget its own color. The screen hung crooked; one hinge busted. He gave it a nudge with his foot. It swung wide with a dry squeal.

He stepped inside and held his breath out of habit.

The air was thick with old cigarette smoke, cheap perfume, and the sour bite of something sweet gone bad—maybe stale alcohol soaked into the carpet, or the bottom of a glass left out too long. The TV was on, low volume, stuck in a marathon of old crime shows. The glow cast pale shadows across the room.

His mom was there. Kind of.

Slouched sideways on the couch, one arm dangled off the edge, cigarette barely clinging to her fingers. Her mouth hung open slightly, lips dry. Ashes dotted her shirt like snowflakes that didn't melt.

The ashtray on the table was full. So was the second one beside it.

"Ma," A.V. said softly, not expecting a response.

Nothing. Just the buzz of the TV and the wet, rattling hum of the old fridge down the hall.

He walked past her and into the kitchen. Flies hovered near the sink. Dishes stacked like Jenga, some with water, most without. A half-empty bag of chips on the counter. Empty cans. No groceries.

He opened the fridge. Closed it again.

Back to the hallway. Step around the creaky floorboard. Duck past the peeling wallpaper.

A.V. closed the door to his room and turned the lock.
Click.
That small sound—the only part of his life he could control.

He turned on the box fan by the window. It rattled like it always did, a familiar hum he could pretend was something softer—like wind, or quiet, or peace.

Then he lay down on the mattress, face to the ceiling, arms crossed over his chest like a question he didn't know how to answer.

The yelling had stopped hours ago, but it was still in him.
Still echoing.

Not a fight between two people—just one voice, bouncing off empty walls.
His mom, pacing the living room, yelling at someone who wasn't there.
Or maybe at herself. Or the silence. Or the memory of what used to be.

It was always worse when she was high.
She'd talk like she was in the middle of an argument no one else could hear—words slurred with rage, questions aimed at the air, accusations fired at ghosts.

He remembered pressing his pillow tight to his ears, trying to block it out.
Not the sound—he could handle that.

It was the pain behind it. The way her voice cracked like something inside her was breaking apart.

The fan blew stale air across his arms, but he didn't move.
Didn't speak.
Didn't cry.

He just waited for the world to go still again.

After a while, he reached under the bed and pulled out the worn note-book—edges curled, corners softened by time.

His headphones were wrapped around it like they'd been sleeping there too. He untangled them slowly, slid them over his ears, and hit play on the old MP3 player tucked in the front pouch of his golden hoodie.

Then he put the headphones on, and the beat kicked in.

Heavy. Dark. Familiar.

He picked up the notebook and uncapped a pen with his teeth.

He turned the music up.

And started to write.

The old fan in the window clicked every three seconds—just loud enough to be annoying, but not loud enough to fix.

Kristin ignored it. She always did.

She stood barefoot in her kitchen, stirring grits in a battered pot, slow and steady like she'd done a thousand mornings before. The scent of butter, salt, and quiet determination filled the tiny apartment. A gospel station played low from the radio on the windowsill—some choir out of Mississippi wailing about valleys and victory.

She hummed with them; lips pressed together.

The stove light flickered overhead. She made a mental note to change the bulb, knowing full well she wouldn't.

The landlord hadn't come by in months, and even if he did, she'd rather fix it herself than hear him breathing heavy and calling her *"mama"* like they were family.

She set out two bowls.

Not because someone was coming.
But because someone might.

Kristin had always cooked too much. Said it was better to be ready for love than surprised by loneliness. Sometimes someone from church would drop by. Sometimes a neighbor. Sometimes nobody at all.

But every time she stirred that pot, she thought of Avery.

Avery, with those big, watchful eyes.
Avery, with his mama's silence and his daddy's temper.
Avery, who hadn't called in two weeks.

She didn't blame him. Not really.

His mother was the type of woman who knew how to break her own heart before anyone else could. And his father—well, some men leave without walking out the door.

Kristin sighed and turned off the burner. The smell of hot grits lingered, rich and warm, but she wasn't hungry anymore.

She walked to the table, cracked open her Bible, and slid her reading glasses on. They sat crooked—one arm bent, the other missing a screw—but they worked.

She didn't read the words. Just looked at the page.

Then she bowed her head.

"Lord," she whispered. "Keep that boy safe. Please. I know you hear me even when I'm too tired to shout. If you can't reach him, send someone who can. Let him feel loved—just once today. That's all I ask."

She stayed like that for a long moment.

The fan clicked again.

And somewhere, far away from the warmth of her kitchen, a butterfly crossed the street under a rising moon.

Kristin stood slowly from the table, joints aching in a way that told the truth better than any mirror ever could.

She moved to the window and peeled the curtain back with two fingers. Outside, the city was soft with dusk. Streetlights blinked awake. A group of teens laughed loud down the block, chasing each other with water bottles. A baby cried two floors up. Somewhere, music played—a lazy, looped beat from a car with more bass than engine.

She watched the world like she was waiting for something.

Not a miracle. She didn't pray for miracles.
Just... signs.

A knock. A phone call. A shadow with her grandson's shoulders.

But the street stayed quiet. So she let the curtain fall.

Back in the living room, a framed photo of her daughter sat on the shelf—back when she smiled with all her teeth and wore gold bangles like armor. Kristin picked it up and ran her thumb across the glass. She didn't cry. Not anymore. Just closed her eyes and let the ache speak in her chest like an old radio tuned to static.

"I should've done more," she whispered.

Then, quieter: "But I did what I could."

She turned the photo down gently, not out of shame—but out of grief fatigue. Sometimes even memory weighs too much.

In the hallway, the phone sat silent on the wall. Beige plastic, coiled cord. She stared at it, daring it to ring.

When it didn't, she walked to the stove, grabbed both bowls of grits, and spooned them into Tupperware. One went in the fridge. The other, the trash.

She washed the pot clean and set it on the rack upside down—water dripping like a slow metronome.

That's when she saw it.

A butterfly on the outside of the kitchen window.

Wings spread wide. Still. Like it had nowhere better to be.

Kristin smiled, soft and tired.

"Alright," she said to no one, "I hear you."

Brent adjusted the collar of his uniform jacket, then looked at himself in the locker room mirror—not to admire, but to check.

Badge: straight.
Duty belt: snug.
Vest: centered.
Eyes… trying not to show how nervous he was.

He wasn't scared, exactly. Just *aware*. That sharp kind of energy you get before doing something that might change you forever.

Behind him, the locker room buzzed with the usual morning chaos. Radios crackled. Boots hit tile. Someone argued with a vending machine. Another cursed into his coffee like it was a hostile witness.

Brent ignored it all. He adjusted his collar. Rolled his shoulders. Bounced once on his heels.

First solo patrol.

Not a ride-along. Not training wheels.
Him, in the cruiser.
Call signs.
Responsibility.
People looking at him like he was the authority.

He exhaled through his nose, steady and slow, the way his dad had taught him.

"Look like a tree. Think like a mountain," his dad always said.
Captain Brooks—retired now, but still casting a long shadow.

Brent didn't want to wear his father's shoes.

He wanted to *earn* them.

A knock on the locker beside him broke his focus.

"Lose the stiffness, rookie," said Officer Delgado—twenty years on the job, permanently unimpressed.
"You look like you slept in a rulebook."

Brent cracked a smile. "Just making sure I've got it right."

Delgado snorted. "It's never all right. This job'll shake the shine off you fast enough."

Kind words, in their own sideways way.

Brent nodded. "Appreciate it."

Delgado walked off, muttering something about rookies and heartburn.

Brent grabbed his thermos, zipped his jacket all the way up, and headed for the garage.

The cruiser was already waiting, humming like a dog that knew it was time to run.

Brent eased into the driver's seat, adjusted the radio, and keyed in his call sign like he'd practiced a hundred times.

"Unit 43, clear for patrol."

Dispatch confirmed.

And just like that—
he was rolling.

First day. First beat.

First step into the life he'd been chasing since he was twelve and saw his father stop a fight at the park just by showing up.

The streets were quiet this morning. Sunlight filtered through the windshield in stripes, and everything had that weird, early clarity— where even the cracks in the sidewalks looked cleaner. He passed a school zone. A couple of kids waved at the cruiser. He waved back, grinning.

This is why he signed up.

Not for the gun. Not for the badge. For this.

To keep good people safe.

To make neighborhoods feel like neighborhoods again.

He drove slower than he needed to. Observing. Respectful. Present.

At the corner of 18th and Hayes, an old man swept his porch, pausing only to tip his head in a nod. Brent nodded back.

The world felt right.

Until the call came in.

"Unit 43, possible domestic at 712 Grand Avenue. Caller states there's yelling, possibly a child crying. No weapons mentioned."

Brent's fingers tightened on the wheel.

"43 responding."

Grand Avenue was only five minutes away, but the tone of the day had already shifted.

The house was one of those sagging two-flats—gray siding, chain-link fence wrapped in rust. A Big Wheel lay on its side in the yard. One window was open, a torn sheet hanging out like a flag of surrender.

He stepped out slowly, radio on his belt, hand near—not on—his weapon. No sirens. No lights.

Just approach.

He knocked once. Then again.

A woman opened the door. Thin. Eyes dark-circled. Maybe early 30s, but she looked older. She held the door with one hand and her jaw like it hurt.

"We're fine," she said flatly.

"Ma'am," Brent said gently, "we got a call. Just want to make sure everyone's okay."

"Nobody called," she replied, too fast.

Behind her, a child peeked around the corner. Maybe six. Wearing a superhero costume two sizes too small.

Brent smiled softly. "Hey, buddy."

The kid didn't answer.

There was a moment—just a breath—where Brent felt it.

The lie.

The woman's body was blocking the doorway too deliberately. She wouldn't meet his eyes. And behind her, on the wall, something was broken. A picture frame? A lamp?

"I just need to come in and make sure everything's alright."

"You got a warrant?" she snapped, voice sharpening.

"No, ma'am. But if someone's hurt—"

"We're FINE."

The kid flinched at her tone.

Brent stepped back, hands raised. He wasn't going to force it. No cause yet. No proof. Just a gut feeling.

He would write down the address. Log the visit. File the report the way he was taught.

But as he walked back to his cruiser, he could still feel the child's eyes on him.

Brent sat in the cruiser with the engine running and the windows down, parked near the edge of a park he used to play in as a kid. A few teenagers shot hoops at the far end of the court; trash talk bouncing with the ball. A mom pushed a stroller nearby, earbuds in, lips moving like she was rapping silently to herself.

Everything looked... normal.

And maybe that's what bothered him the most.

The call at Grand Avenue—it had ended without incident. No arrest. No shouting match. No dramatic standoff. Just a door, a lie, and a little boy in a costume who didn't say a word.

Brent stared at the report on his tablet for a long time before finally typing:
No visible injuries. Resident denied wrongdoing. No further action taken.

He hated typing that.

He hated how neat it looked.

Because he *knew* something was off. Felt it in the way the woman clutched the doorframe. Saw it in the boy's shoulders. In the way he didn't wave back.

Still, protocol was protocol. His training officer would've said: "You did your job."
But Brent wasn't here to just *do his job*. He was here to help people. To protect them.

"Fat lotta good that did," he muttered to himself.

"Talking to the wind, rookie?"

The voice came from behind the open driver's side door. Brent looked up to see Delgado, leaning against the side of the cruiser with a paper cup of gas station coffee in one hand and a scuffed-up smirk in the other.

"Domestic on Grand," Brent said. "You ever get one where you know something's wrong, but there's nothing you can do?"

Delgado snorted. "You just described half the job."

Brent didn't laugh.

Delgado sipped his coffee and shrugged. "You'll learn. Sometimes you help. Sometimes you show up too late. And sometimes... you're just there to witness the wreckage."

He tapped the side of the car.

"But showing up still matters."

Then he walked off.

Brent looked back at the screen. The boy's face flashed through his mind again—painted with shadows and silence.

He tapped the report once. Closed it.

Then drove on.

Brent's boots hit the hardwood floor with a soft thunk.

He kicked them off by the door—quietly, out of habit—and stepped into the living room where low lamp light spilled across the couch, a folded blanket, and a baby bottle half-full of formula. The house smelled like vanilla lotion and faintly of baby powder. Something peaceful. Something human.

He heard her humming before he saw her.

Lena.

Curled up on the loveseat with Uziel pressed to her chest, rocking gently. Their baby had a full head of dark hair and his father's nose—sleepy and milk-drunk, curled like a comma against her collarbone.

"You're late," she whispered, without looking up.

"I know," Brent said, lowering himself onto the armrest beside her. "It was a long one."

She looked up at him then—those same eyes he fell for in high school bio, the ones that lit up even while dissecting mice. The ones that still made his chest tighten.

"You good?"

Brent nodded. "Yeah. Just... a call. Nothing happened. But it stuck."

He rubbed the back of his neck, then leaned in and kissed Uziel's forehead. The baby sighed in his sleep, one tiny hand curling toward the sky like a question he hadn't learned to ask yet.

"What kind of call?" Lena asked gently.

Brent didn't answer right away.

"Domestic," he said finally. "No proof. Just instinct."

Lena reached out and took his hand.

"You'll get better at knowing when to push," she said.

"That's not what scares me," he replied.

She tilted her head. "Then what?"

"That one day," he said, voice low, "I'll stop feeling it. That I'll show up, hear a lie, and just move on. Not because I believe them... but because it's easier."

Lena didn't speak right away. She just shifted, making room, and he slid down onto the couch beside her.

"You won't," she said. "You're not built like that."

He didn't answer.

Because some small, gnawing part of him already wondered if he might be.

They sat there in silence for a while—baby breathing softly between them, the world outside settling into night. Brent leaned his head back against the couch and stared at the ceiling, eyes tracing a water stain shaped like a crooked heart.

He wanted to believe her.

But the job had a way of pressing in—not all at once, but in little, invisible places.

And something inside him already felt a little heavier than it had that morning.

Lena adjusted Uziel gently, tucking the blanket up to his chin. He let out a tiny grunt and curled tighter into her chest, perfectly content in a world he didn't yet know was broken.

Brent watched them and felt a strange ache.
Not sadness.
Not joy either.
Something in between—like awe wearing a tired coat.

"He looks like you," he said.

Lena scoffed. "He's got your nose and your resting cop face."

"I do not have a resting cop face."

"You absolutely do."

Brent laughed, quiet and breathy, like he didn't want to wake the baby or the moment.

Lena leaned into him, shoulder against his.

"Do you ever wish you'd picked something else?" she asked. "Like... teacher? Firefighter? Accountant?"

He thought about that.

"No," he said. "Not yet."

"But maybe one day?"

He nodded.

She didn't press further. That was Lena—knew when to poke and when to let it sit.

"Your dad called," she said after a beat. "Left a message. Said to tell you not to 'overthink every damn shadow.' Whatever that means."

Brent exhaled through his nose. "It means he still thinks I'm soft."

"He doesn't think that."

"He does. But that's okay. I'd rather be soft than stone."

Lena looked up at him. "Soft things last longer. Stone crumbles."

He smiled at that. Kissed her hair. Let the quiet stretch again.

The house ticked around them—pipes shifting, fridge buzzing, the occasional click from the baseboard heater. Domestic music.

"Do you think he'll remember this?" Brent asked, looking down at Uziel.

"No. But we will."

And something about that hit him deep—like her voice was a string tied around his chest, keeping him tethered to something he wasn't even sure how to name yet.

He wanted to be the kind of father who protected without becoming distant. Who could look into darkness without carrying it home. Who didn't mistake silence for strength.

He kissed Uziel's forehead again.

"I'll keep you safe," he whispered.

And meant it.

Even if the job would spend the next decade trying to prove him wrong.

A.V. leaned against the brick wall behind Rico's bodega, hoodie up, eyes scanning the street like he had somewhere to be—like he belonged out there.

Rico had run the place since before A.V. could spell "bodega." Always said hello, always told the kids to stay in school, even when they rolled their eyes and grabbed chips they didn't pay for. He didn't sell respect—but he earned it.

A.V. was pushing fourteen, all limbs and late-night thoughts, still waiting for his voice to decide if it was gonna stay low or squeak one more time.

His sneakers were scuffed, his jeans a little too short, and the notebook stuffed in his hoodie pocket

was the only thing he didn't borrow from somebody else.

It was a Tuesday. Late spring. Warm but not hot. The kind of day where school felt optional, and the world outside seemed more honest anyway.

He wasn't going back. Not today. Maybe not tomorrow either.

Inside the bodega, Rico's cousin Devon was stocking shelves and throwing glances through the window.

"You just gonna lean there lookin' tragic, or you gonna do somethin'?"

"I'm doin' plenty," A.V. replied.

Devon rolled his eyes. "Yeah, you writin' them sadboy raps in your head again? You better spit somethin' hot or go get a job, bro."

A.V. didn't answer. He pulled the notebook out, flipped to a page halfway back, and started scribbling. A line he'd heard in a dream last night. Something about broken clocks and bruised promises. He couldn't shake it.

He'd been writing more lately. Not just rhymes, but verses. Full songs. Stuff he'd never show anybody except maybe Malik—who told him his bars were "mid but gettin' better."

The thing was... they weren't really for anybody else.

They were armor.

Paper-thin, pen-sharp protection from the silence he carried inside.

He still remembered those last few days with his mom.
How she stopped speaking.
Just drifted past him like she was stuck in a trance—eyes cloudy, skin drawn, moving like her body remembered how but her mind wasn't quite there. Always either asleep or chasing sleep.
The woman who used to hum Tupac while folding his socks couldn't even remember what day it was.

And Grandma Kristin? She was trying. But A.V. could feel the fear under her smile. Like she knew he was slipping—not gone, but going.

Devon stepped outside, holding a bag of chips and a soda.

"You eat today?"

A.V. shrugged.

"Take it," Devon said, tossing him the bag.

A.V. caught it, stared for a second. "You know I ain't got money."

"Who said anything about money?"

He hesitated—then took the chips, eyes low. "Thanks."

Devon didn't say anything else. Just walked back inside.

And A.V. sat down on the milk crate near the dumpster, opened the soda with a slow hiss, and watched the world pass him by. Buses. Bikes. Moms yelling at kids. Laughter. Sirens. Music somewhere distant.

He pulled the notebook back out, flipped to a blank page, and wrote:

I used to be somebody's reason to get clean.
Now I'm just a shadow with a sixteen.

He didn't know if it was good.

He just knew it was true.

The front door creaked louder than usual.

A.V. slipped inside, shoes off out of habit, and closed it behind him with a soft click. He could smell it before he saw her—citrus cleaner and onions, the signature scent of Kristin's kitchen.

She was at the stove again, even though it was almost dark. Pot simmering low, the hum of her gospel station barely audible over the rattle of the fan in the window. She didn't look up.

"You skipped school again," she said, voice calm but heavy.

"I ain't skip. I just… redirected my energy," A.V. muttered.

"That supposed to be clever?"

He walked past her to the fridge. Opened it. Looked. Closed it again. Just like always.

She turned down the burner and finally faced him. Her hands were on her hips. She wore that old floral apron she never threw out, the one with the burn mark near the pocket. Her gray was showing more in her roots. Her eyes were tired—but sharp as ever.

"You out there makin' music, or just runnin' wild?"

A.V. didn't answer.

She stepped closer. "Avery."

He flinched a little. She hardly ever used his full name unless something sacred was coming.

"I been good," he said. "Ain't doin' nothin' crazy."

"That ain't what I asked."

He dropped onto the old loveseat with a sigh. "I'm not out here robbin' folks, Grandma. I just... I don't feel right at school. Feels fake. Feels like I'm in a movie where I ain't got a script."

Kristin sat down across from him at the table, rubbing her knees. "You think the rest of us got a script? You think I wanted to be raisin' another baby at sixty-something years old while my daughter out there drownin' in her own sorrow?"

That stung. He looked away.

"I'm not tryna be a burden—"

"You ain't a burden," she cut in, firm. "You're my boy. But baby… you can't just drift. That world out there'll eat you if you don't plant your feet. And I already lost one child to the current."

He swallowed hard. His notebook felt like it weighed a thousand pounds in his hoodie pocket.

"I ain't her," he whispered.

Kristin's face softened. She stood, crossed the room, and sat next to him. Placed her hand on his knee.

"I know. But you *her son*. And that means you got her fire… and maybe some of her ghosts too. But you don't gotta carry 'em alone."

A long pause.

Then she added, almost as an afterthought: "You eat today?"

He nodded slowly. "Devon gave me some chips."

She smirked. "That boy still frontin' snacks like he got a job?"

A.V. smiled. Just barely. "Said I looked tragic."

"He ain't wrong," she said, brushing hair from his forehead. "But you mine. So you better be tragic with a full stomach."

She got up and went back to the stove.

He watched her move—steady, proud, like nothing could touch her. Not the bills on the counter. Not the pain in her knees. Not even the fear she tried to hide every time he came home late.

He pulled out his notebook.

Didn't write a rhyme.

Just one sentence.

I think she's the reason I haven't disappeared yet.

That night, A.V. dreamed of water.

Not an ocean—a flood. Rising in a living room with peeling wallpaper and dirty dishes floating past. His mother stood waist-deep in it, lighting a cigarette that wouldn't catch. Her eyes were empty, mouth moving without sound. She didn't even look at him.

Kristin was in the hallway, hands cupped like she was trying to scoop the water out with her palms, one gospel hymn on repeat like a broken lullaby.

"I told you, baby," she said. "Don't let it pull you under."

But he was already sinking.

The water was cold. It didn't splash. It whispered.

Every name he'd ever been called. Every mistake he didn't mean to make. Every look that told him he wasn't enough. It filled his ears, his lungs, his thoughts.

And then, through the murk—a butterfly.

Glowing. Silent. Floating just out of reach.

He reached for it.

And woke up with tears in his eyes.

Kristin was asleep on the couch, mouth slightly open, the TV humming static over a dead-end talk show rerun.

The whole apartment breathed in shallow rhythms—clock ticking, fridge groaning, the distant sound of a siren stretched thin by distance.

A.V. sat on the edge of his mattress, staring at the floor.

There was a weight in his chest that writing couldn't shake. A pressure behind the ribs that whispered things like: You ain't built for this world. You ain't got no place. You ain't even got your name on nothing.

He tried to ignore it.

But tonight, it was too loud.

The house he walked to wasn't familiar—but it wasn't random either.

It was one of those places kids whispered about.

Empty. Half-burnt. Half-owned.

Windows boarded. Roof sagging like tired shoulders.

A place where time had stopped.

The storm had been building all day.

Now it cracked above him like a warning he couldn't hear.

Rain pelted the sidewalk. Lightning lit up the clouds like x-rays of heaven.

He didn't hesitate.

He walked through the broken door, up the splintered stairs, and out onto the roof.

It wasn't high.

Four stories. Maybe less.

But it was enough.

The ledge was narrow.

Crumbled brick.

One misstep and gravity would decide the rest.

He stood there, soaked through.
Arms down. Shoulders trembling—not from cold, but from every-thing **he couldn't hold anymore.**
He didn't cry.
Didn't scream.
Just stared into the distance like he was waiting for the world to confirm what he already believed:

You don't matter.
You were just something someone left behind.

Earlier that night, Brent sat in his cruiser outside a shuttered gas station, windows half-down, sipping lukewarm coffee that tasted more like burnt rubber than caffeine.

The streets were quiet, but not calm.

A stillness that didn't sit right.

The kind that feels like holding your breath.

His radio crackled to life.

"Unit 24, possible 10-56. Caller reported a boy on the roof at 836 Greenfield. No threats, but said it 'looked wrong.'"

No caller ID. No details.

Brent's hand froze above the gearshift.

"24 en route," he replied, voice steady, though his heart had already started to race.

Greenfield.

That was one of the blocks people didn't bother calling back from— if they called at all.

He flipped on the headlights, not the sirens.

Didn't want to spook whoever was up there.

As he turned onto Greenfield, the city felt like it shrank.

The street narrowed. The trees leaned in too close. The air got thick.

He rolled past 832… 834… 836.

The house sat like a forgotten breath.

Porch sagging. Windows black.

One loose gutter banging softly in the wind.

Then he saw it.

A silhouette on the roof.

Small.

Still.

Too still.

———— 🦋 ————

He parked two houses down. Radioed in.

"Unit 24 on scene. Possible juvenile on roof. Approaching on foot."

He stepped out.

Didn't slam the door.

Didn't touch his belt.

Didn't think about protocol.

He just walked toward the house, slow and open-palmed,

because this wasn't a call for backup.

This was a call for presence.

The rain came harder now.

The stairs inside groaned like they didn't want anyone to reach him.

When Brent emerged on the roof, he didn't speak at first.

Didn't want to scare him.

The boy—skinny, drenched, maybe fifteen—stood near the edge, hoodie stuck to his arms like skin.

Lightning flashed.

Brent didn't move.

A.V.'s voice cracked:

"She don't even know where I'm at. My grandma."

"She'd rather you be lost than gone."

A.V. closed his eyes.

"I don't know how to fix this."

"You don't have to," Brent said.

"You just have to stay. One more minute. Then another."

Another beat.

Another breath.

Then—

A.V. stepped back from the edge.

Just one step.

But it was everything.

He dropped to his knees, collapsed into himself.

Brent moved in—careful, slow—and placed a hand on the boy's shoulder.

Not as a cop.

Not as a hero.

Just as a man who knew what it meant to stand in the rain and feel like it was all too heavy.

———— 🦋 ————

The cruiser rolled down the backroads, slow and steady, like it knew not to rush this.

A.V. sat in the passenger seat, hoodie pulled low, notebook wedged between his knee and the door. He didn't speak. Didn't move much either. Just stared out the window like the city had turned into a slideshow of memories he didn't want to remember.

Brent drove with one hand on the wheel, the other resting on the gearshift. The radio was silent now. He'd turned it off after calling in the welfare check.

He wasn't ready for the world to speak again. Not yet.

The only sound in the car was the occasional thump of a loose soda bottle rolling under the seat, and the squeak of leather whenever Brent shifted.

"You hungry?" Brent asked finally, voice gentle.

A.V. nodded, barely.

"There's a spot up on Ashland. Place called Tony's. Old-school. Cheap waffles. Good bacon."

A long pause.

Then A.V. said, almost inaudible, "You really eat there in uniform?"

"Every time I want to remember I'm still human," Brent said.

That earned him a tiny smirk. Barely visible. But it was there.

They passed a mural painted across the side of a building—faded fists raised skyward, names written in the clouds. One of them was crossed out in red spray paint.

A.V. watched it vanish in the rearview mirror.

"I didn't think anybody'd come," he said after a while.

"You didn't ask," Brent replied.

"I didn't think I mattered enough to."

That landed hard between them.

Brent didn't rush to fill the silence.

He turned onto a quieter street, lined with shuttered storefronts and flickering neon signs. Ahead, a soft golden glow spilled from a squat brick building with an old red awning and peeling white letters: TONY'S.

The place looked like it hadn't changed since the '80s. That's what made it perfect.

Brent pulled into the side lot, turned off the engine, and looked over.

A.V. didn't move.

Brent didn't pressure.

Finally, A.V. muttered, "I don't got money."

"Didn't ask you to pay," Brent said, already opening his door.

They stepped out together.

Not cop and suspect.

Just two souls trying not to fall apart.

Tony's smelled like it always did—griddle grease, cinnamon, old coffee, and survival.

The bell over the door gave a lazy jingle as Brent and A.V. stepped in. The floor tiles were cracked in just the right places to feel familiar, and the booths were wrapped in red vinyl worn to a dull shine. A jukebox in the corner blinked with blues tracks no one ever touched. The counter guy gave Brent a nod without saying a word.

They took a booth near the window. A.V. slid in with his hands in his lap, eyes scanning the laminated menu like it held ancient secrets.

"Get whatever," Brent said, dropping the menu on the table. "But if you don't get waffles, I'm judging you."

A.V. cracked half a grin. "What if I'm more of a pancakes guy?"

"Then you're under arrest."

That pulled a real smile, faint but whole.

Tony shuffled over—balding, pot-bellied, with a mustache like it was grown for respect alone.

"Same for you, Officer Brooks?"

"Yeah, and throw in a plate for my friend here."

Tony looked at A.V., didn't flinch, didn't pry. Just nodded.

"Two waffle specials. Coffee and orange juice?"

"Perfect."

Tony disappeared like a ghost behind the counter, leaving them in the hush of humming lights and quiet clinks of forks on plates from the other side of the room.

A.V. stared at the napkin dispenser.

"You always like this?" he asked.

"Like what?"

"Calm."

Brent sipped his water. "Only when it counts."

A.V. picked at a sugar packet, silent for a beat.

"I thought cops were supposed to yell. Grab people. Call backup."

"You didn't need backup," Brent said. "You needed someone to sit down."

That hit hard. A.V. looked away. His eyes were glassy again, but he blinked it down fast.

"You ever want to just... disappear?" he asked.

Brent looked at him carefully. Not with pity. Not with fear.

"Yeah," he said. "Plenty of times. But I realized if I disappeared, I'd miss things I didn't even know were coming."

A.V. looked up.

"Like what?"

The plates landed in front of them with a soft clatter.

Golden waffles, thick-cut bacon, scrambled eggs, steam rising in soft ribbons.

Brent smiled. "Like this."

A.V. stared at the food like it was a language he hadn't heard in a while.

He picked up his fork.

The first bite of waffle stuck to the syrup like a memory that didn't want to let go.

The sky was still dark when they pulled away from Tony's, headlights casting long, soft cones over cracked pavement.

The city was sleeping lighter now—early morning traffic just starting to stir. A jogger passed on the sidewalk, hoodie up, earbuds in. A man unlocked a bakery down the block and propped the door with a chair.

A.V. sat in the passenger seat again, but he wasn't shrinking this time. He had one leg pulled up under him, head resting lightly against the glass. The heat was on just enough to keep the windows from fogging.

Brent didn't say much.

Didn't have to.

The silence was different now.

Less empty.

A.V. broke it.

"I saw a clock in that house," he said.

Brent glanced over, then back to the road. "Yeah?"

"It was ticking. But the hands weren't moving."

Brent nodded slowly. "Broken?"

"I guess. But it was still makin' noise. Like it wanted people to think it was workin'."

He paused.

"Felt like me."

Brent didn't respond right away. Just let the road stretch.

Then: "I've got an old pocket watch at home. Belonged to my dad. Doesn't work either."

A.V. looked over, eyebrows raised. "Why keep it?"

"Because it reminds me…" Brent said, "that none of the stuff we chase matters more than right now. Right this moment. Time doesn't have to move to matter."

A.V. stared out the window again.

"Didn't think cops got deep."

"Only the good ones."

Another beat of quiet.

"You think I'm gonna be okay?" A.V. asked, voice small.

Brent didn't look at him this time. Just kept his eyes on the road.

"I think you already are," he said. "You made it to tomorrow."

They pulled into the back lot of the station.

The lights buzzed overhead, cold and white.

Brent didn't park near the holding cells. He parked far off, near the side door, where it was quiet. No noise. No uniforms coming and going. Just a patch of space where the world could stay still a little longer.

A.V. looked at the building. Then at Brent.

"Do I gotta go in the back?"

"No," Brent said gently. "You're not in trouble."

He unlocked the doors.

"We're just gonna talk. Maybe call someone. Make sure you've got options. People who care."

A.V. hesitated. His hand hovered near the door handle.

"I thought I was gonna die tonight," he whispered.

Brent didn't flinch. "Me too."

A.V. finally stepped out.

And Brent walked beside him—not behind, not ahead.

Just with him.

A.V. didn't talk much after that night.

Not to the counselor the station brought in. Not to the officer who took down his information. Not even to Kristin—not right away.

But a week later, she found him at the kitchen table.

Headphones in.

Writing.

Sunlight warmed the crown of his head while his hand moved fast across the page. A full verse. Then another. Then silence, as he read it back to himself and crossed half of it out. He was building, not just venting.

She didn't say anything. Just slid a plate of eggs next to him and kissed the top of his head.

"I got you, baby," she whispered.

Six months later, a flyer showed up on the station bulletin board— taped over an old recruitment poster, crooked and low-tech.

Local Youth Showcase – Spoken Word Night
@ Gardenview Library – Community Room
Featuring performances by: Malik, Tamika, and A.V.

Brent stared at it for a long moment.
Didn't pull it down.

Didn't tell anyone he knew one of the names.
He just left it there.
Letting the ripple carry on.

Somewhere across town, streetlights blinked into existence one by one, like tired stars returning to work.

A.V. sat on the steps outside his building, notebook open, pen tapping slow. Not writing yet. Just… listening.

To the city.

To the space between things.

Behind him, Kristin was cooking again—same gospel station humming in the kitchen, same worn floorboard squeaking beneath her sway.

And a few blocks away, Brent drove the same loop he always did, same roads, same corners. But something felt different. He couldn't explain it, not even to himself.

It was the kind of shift you don't notice until much later—when you look back and realize that night was the one where something deep inside you started to change.

Where hope didn't win.

But it didn't lose either.

The Boy Made of Light

A butterfly's wings don't contain color—they bend light. The brilliance we see is not pigment, but reflection. It's not what they are. It's how they're seen. And that's what makes them beautiful.

U ziel was five years old the first time his teacher called him "sunshine."

Not because he smiled all the time—he didn't.

But because even when he was quiet, the room seemed warmer with him in it.

He was the kind of kid who gave away his snack if someone forgot theirs, then turned it into a joke so they wouldn't feel bad. Who asked questions like, *"Can spiders miss people?"* and *"Why can't we see love?"*

He didn't know it yet, but people were starting to orbit him.

He had a habit of waking up before everyone else.

Not because he had to.

Because he liked the quiet.

The first light of morning slipping through his curtains. The house still and half-asleep. It made him feel like he had the whole world to himself—just for a little while.

Sometimes he'd sneak into the kitchen to make "breakfast" for the family. Mostly toast. Occasionally disaster. Once, at age seven, he microwaved eggs in a paper bowl. The bowl caught fire. He cried—not because of the flames, but because he thought he'd disappointed his mom.

Lena came running, heart pounding. When she saw the smoldering mess, she should've yelled.

Instead, she pulled him in and held him tight.

"Why were you even trying to cook, Z?"

"I wanted to make you happy."

"You already do," she said, tears in her voice.

He didn't forget that. Ever.

At school, he wasn't the loudest. Or the smartest. Or the fastest—though he *was* fast. That boy could run like he had something chasing him, even if it was just his own shadow.

But what people remembered was how he made them feel.

When Mia broke her glasses, Uziel offered her his sunglasses and called her "Agent M."

When Theo got picked last in gym, Uziel traded teams just to even the odds—and made it sound like it was his idea all along.

He didn't like bullies.

But he didn't fight them.

He **outloved** them.

Made kindness look like strength.

And for some reason, it worked.

At home, his little sister trailed him like a second heartbeat. She called him "Uzi," and he let her, even though no one else was allowed to.

He told her bedtime stories about a superhero named *The Crimson Nova*, who fought crime using art and hugs instead of violence. She drew him in crayons—always with a cape, always with Uziel's eyes.

"You think I'll be as brave as you someday?" she asked once, already halfway asleep.

"Braver," he whispered.

It was the spring concert.

Third grade.

Cafeteria turned auditorium.

Folding chairs packed tight, parents elbow to elbow, programs clutched like nervous shields.

The stage was decorated with cardboard flowers and construction paper butterflies, some of which had already started peeling off the wall. The school's attempt at whimsy.

Backstage, the kids were buzzing—tugging at their shirts, checking their laces, whispering and giggling in bursts.

Except for one boy.

Jordan.

He stood near the edge of the curtain, frozen. Hands clenched at his sides, eyes wide. Like a statue that still remembered how to be scared.

Uziel saw him.

Walked up quiet, like he always did when something mattered.

"You good?" he asked.

Jordan shook his head.

"I can't," he whispered. "I can't go out there. Everyone's lookin'. I'll mess up. I'll forget the words."

Uziel thought about it for a second.

Then he shrugged. "Okay. So we forget the words together."

Jordan blinked.

"What?"

"Yeah," Uziel said. "If you mess up, I'll mess up too. That way you won't be alone."

He offered his hand.

Jordan didn't take it right away. But Uziel didn't pull it back either.

And when their teacher called their row to the stage, Jordan reached out—tentative, shaking—and held on.

They walked out together, hand in hand.

Jordan didn't let go.

Neither did Uziel.

And when the music started, and the crowd leaned forward in that collective hush, Uziel wasn't looking at the audience.

He was watching Jordan.

Mouthing the words.

Smiling like it was no big deal.

And when Jordan finally opened his mouth and began to sing—quiet but steady, voice trembling on the first line—Uziel gave him the slightest nod.

You're doing it.
You're okay.

The concert went on. The song ended. Applause filled the room.

Jordan looked like he'd just run a marathon and flown at the same time.

After the show, a woman in the crowd whispered, "Did you see that little boy help the other one?"

Lena heard it. So did Brent.

They didn't say anything.

They just looked at each other.

And in Brent's chest, something swelled that had nothing to do with pride.

It was gratitude.

That somehow, *this kid had come from him.*

The car ride home was quiet in the way all good things are.

Uziel had knocked out five minutes in—head tilted against the window, mouth slightly open, a smudge of chocolate cupcake still on his cheek. His sister sat next to him, quieter now. Still humming, but slower, softer—like even the melody was getting sleepy. Her legs swung a little, then stilled.

Brent drove.

Lena watched the kids in the rearview mirror, her smile soft but far away.

"Did you see him?" she asked finally, voice low so it wouldn't wake them.

"I saw him," Brent said.

They didn't need to say who they meant.

Lena turned toward the window, eyes glinting in the amber blur of passing streetlights. "He just... knows what people need. I don't know how. I didn't teach him that."

"Maybe you didn't have to," Brent said.

A few more beats passed in soft hums and tire noise.

Then Lena asked, "Do you ever get scared? That we'll screw it up?"

Brent didn't answer right away. He focused on the road like it might tell him something.

"All the time," he admitted. "But then he goes and does something like that... and I think maybe we're okay."

Lena nodded.

"Maybe he's here to teach *us* something," she said.

Brent glanced at her. "You think that's how it works?"

"I don't know," she said. "But it feels like it does."

They turned onto their block.

Brent slowed the car as they pulled into the driveway, headlights brushing over the porch like an exhale.

Neither of them moved to wake the kids.

They just sat there a moment longer, the silence warm and alive.

A pause, held between two people who both knew—without saying it—that something precious was unfolding, right in front of them.

It was late on a Saturday, the kind of warm summer night where even the mosquitoes seemed lazy.

Brent had just pulled into the driveway, cruiser rumbling soft as a cat's purr. He didn't even have the key out of the ignition when the front door swung open and Uziel came barreling out barefoot, wearing Spider-Man pajamas and a plastic mask pushed halfway up his forehead.

"Dad! Dad! Did you arrest anybody?"

Brent laughed, leaning across the seat to pop the door open. "Just a raccoon in a trash can. He resisted. Had priors."

Uziel climbed in fast, settling into the passenger seat like he'd trained for it.

"Turn the lights on!"

"You trying to get me fired?"

"Just a little bit?"

Brent reached over and flipped the interior light on instead. Soft glow filled the cab. Uziel leaned forward, tiny fingers dancing across the radio knobs like they were missile controls.

"I bet you could catch *every* bad guy if you had superpowers."

Brent raised an eyebrow. "You think I need powers?"

"Nah," Uziel said, settling back. "You're already kinda like a superhero."

Brent went quiet at that.

There were a lot of days when he didn't feel like a hero. Some nights when the badge felt heavier than the vest. But hearing that from *him*?

That landed somewhere deep.

"You know," Brent said, "when I was your age, I wanted to be a superhero too."

"Yeah, but you got grown-up bills now," Uziel said, deadly serious.

Brent laughed loud. "Truest thing anyone's said all year."

They sat like that for a while, lights on, windows cracked. Not talking. Just being.

Then Brent looked over and said, "You wanna drive?"

Uziel's eyes lit up. "For real?"

"For fake," Brent said, scooting back and letting his son climb into his lap. "But you can still steer."

Uziel grabbed the wheel with both hands, mouth set in a tight little line of focus.

"Where we headed, Captain?" Brent asked.

"To the museum. Gotta stop a jewel thief before midnight."

"Good call."

They sat there ten more minutes, saving the city in their heads.

Then Brent carried his son inside, half-asleep, cape dragging behind them in the moonlight.

Later that night, long after Brent tucked him in, Uziel crept back out of bed.

The house was quiet. Lights low. Only the kitchen lamp left on— Lena's trick for chasing out bad dreams and letting love hang around a little longer.

Uziel climbed into a chair at the kitchen table, legs swinging underneath.

He pulled out his sketchpad. Crayons scattered across the surface like tiny weapons of joy. He didn't rush. He never did. Drawing was sacred.

Line by line, he brought his idea to life.

A superhero in a blue uniform. No cape. No mask. Just a badge and a gentle face.

Next to him—smaller, leaner, younger—a sidekick with a backwards hat and a backpack full of gadgets and poems.

At the top of the page, in big shaky letters, he wrote:

THE GOOD GUYS

And underneath, smaller:

(They always show up.)

He set the crayon down. Stared at the drawing.

Then smiled—small, but real.

He didn't know why, but tonight felt *safe*.

The Space
Between Notes

A butterfly flaps its wings, and nothing happens—at first. But
the air shifts. The pressure changes. A ripple begins in silence
long before the storm ever arrives. The smallest motion
doesn't always make noise. But it always leaves a mark.

Brent missed the green light again.

He wasn't distracted. Wasn't checking his phone. Just...
forgot to go.

The car behind him honked—long, irritated. He jerked forward like
waking from a dream, hand tightening on the wheel. The light turned
yellow halfway through the intersection.

His jaw clenched. His hands didn't let go of the wheel until he was
parked in his driveway.

The porch light was on. A soft, warm amber glow bleeding onto the
sidewalk. He sat in the cruiser with the engine running, staring at it
like it might blink out if he moved too fast.

Inside the house, shadows passed behind the curtains. Uziel. His daughter. Lena.

A small chorus of voices that used to feel like music.

He turned the engine off, opened the door, and stepped into the evening.

Dinner was ready when he walked in—plates already made, the room already warm. Mashed potatoes. Meatloaf. Something sweet coming from the oven.

Uziel and his sister sat at the table, mid-story, mid-giggle.

"—and then Mr. Lyle tripped over the cord, and the projector hit the floor *again,*" Uziel was saying. "It's like... the fourth time this month."

His sister was howling with laughter. "It made a sound like *BOOMP!*"

Brent tried to smile.

Lena looked over her shoulder. "Hey, baby."

"Hey."

She handed him a plate. Their fingers brushed.

"You good?" she asked quietly.

"Long shift," he replied, without looking at her.

He sat. Ate in slow, quiet bites.

The kids kept talking. Lena kept smiling. But under the table, her foot nudged his gently. Not romantic. Not playful.

Checking his pulse.

Later that night, she found him in the garage.

Just standing there. Not working on anything. Not holding a tool. Just leaning against the workbench, staring at an old box of broken parts he'd been meaning to toss for a year.

She stepped into the frame of the door, arms folded loosely across her chest.

"Brent."

He didn't turn.

"You're doing that thing again," she said.

"What thing?"

"Looking at stuff like it wronged you."

He smiled, barely. "Just tired."

"Is that what you call it now?"

He turned then. Eyes softer. "What do you want me to say, Lena?"

"I don't want you to say anything. I want you to let me in."

She didn't step closer. She knew better.

He nodded once. That careful kind of nod that means *I hear you* but *I'm not ready yet.*

While she brushed her teeth, Brent sat on the edge of the bed. He looked at the floor like it might hold the answer to something.

By the time she came out, he was lying down, one arm over his eyes. The other hand resting lightly on his chest, like he was trying to hold something in place.

She slid in beside him.

Said nothing.

Just let the silence stretch until it stopped feeling like absence and started feeling like a kind of truth.

Brent didn't talk about work at home anymore.

He used to. Early on. Told stories with edge-of-your-seat pacing— storefront standoffs, foot chases, the time a drunk guy climbed a billboard and tried to shout confessions to God. He made it sound like the job was just another kind of adventure.

Back then, Uziel had eaten it up. Every word.

Back then, his daughter would crawl onto his chest during the retell-ings, tracing circles on his collarbone with one finger like she was drawing a badge.

But lately?

Brent came home quieter.

He let the stories stay locked in his chest.

Because the stories had changed.

———— 🦋 ————

As darkness setteled in, he sat on the edge of his daughter's bed, the nightlight casting soft shadows on her bookshelf—little animal figurines, a row of bedtime stories, a drawing Uziel had made of their whole family flying through the sky.

She clutched a plush fox to her chest, eyelids drooping.

"I don't like when you're gone so long," she said softly.

"I know, sweetheart."

"Are you catching the bad guys?"

He paused. "Trying."

"Do you get scared?"

"Sometimes."

She looked at him, wide-eyed.

"But you're brave, right?"

Brent smiled, brushing her hair back. "Only because I have to be."

She yawned. "You're still a good guy."

That one landed hard.

He kissed her forehead. "So are you."

She was asleep a minute later.

He stayed a while longer.

Just watching her breathe.

————— 🦋 —————

In the hallway, he paused outside Uziel's door.

Didn't knock.

Just listened.

Faint scribbles on paper. The occasional sound of a chair creaking. A breath held, then released.

Brent rested his hand on the doorframe.

He used to think his job was to protect his family from the world.

Now, some nights, he wondered if his job was slowly turning him into the thing they'd one day need protection from.

————— 🦋 —————

He stepped outside onto the porch.

Lit a cigarette he didn't want. Let it burn anyway.

The block was quiet. One porch light flickering down the street. Distant music from a car passing on the next avenue. The low, eternal hum of the city just existing.

His hands ached. Not from use. From **holding on too tightly** to things he didn't know how to put down.

There were moments lately when he felt like a passenger in his own body—watching himself respond to calls, fill out reports, nod at things he didn't hear. He wondered if this was what aging felt like: not getting slower, just getting *heavier.*

But then there were nights like this.

When the house was still full of breath and stories and soft voices that didn't need to be told to quiet down.

When Lena's light was still on in the bedroom.

When his daughter dreamed of foxes and magic.

When his son, somewhere upstairs, was still writing poems about **good guys** who show up.

And maybe that was the thing that kept him whole.

Not the badge. Not the job. Not the pride.

But the **belief** his kids still had in him.

He finished the cigarette. Stamped it out. Looked up at the stars, even though they barely showed through the city haze.

Then he went back inside.

And closed the door behind him.

The Weight of Unsaid Things

A butterfly can fly thousands of miles without a sound. Some things travel farther when they're quiet. Especially pain.

A.V. was eight the night his dad got locked up.

But that wasn't when the loss started.

The real loss began years before, in the quiet.

Not the kind of quiet that comes with peace—but the kind that hovers in a room like smoke. The kind that curls into corners, behind doors, between meals.

His father was there—most days. Shoes by the door. Jacket on the chair. A half-drunk beer sweating on the kitchen counter. But his presence was like the old radio in the corner that barely picked up signal: always static, always tuned to something A.V. could never quite hear.

He would come home tired. Always tired. Tired from work, tired from life, tired from things he never talked about.

He wouldn't look A.V. in the eye when he came in.

He'd drop his keys on the table with a sigh that sounded like a warning, not a greeting.

Then he'd sit in front of the TV—volume up, face blank—watching reruns of shows he didn't even like, just for the noise.

A.V. learned early how to move like a shadow.

How to keep footsteps light. How to close cabinets without a sound. How to read his father's mood by the way he sat: shoulders high meant danger, elbows spread meant maybe you could ask for something, hands on his face meant don't.

Once, when he was seven, A.V. drew a picture in class of a superhero that looked like his dad.

Big arms, big badge, big smile.

He'd colored it carefully—red cape, blue sky, gold stars.

He brought it home and waited by the door, picture behind his back, jittery with pride. When his dad walked in, he stepped forward, held it out like a gift.

"Look," he said. "It's you."

His father took it, stared at it for half a second, then set it down on the table without a word.

No smile.

No thank you.

Just a grunt, and the creak of the recliner as he sat down to watch the game.

A.V. stared at the picture for a long time after that—saw how the crayon colors already looked faded in the kitchen light. He picked it up and took it back to his room.

Folded it in half.

Put it in a drawer.

He never drew him again.

There were good moments—if you wanted to believe in them hard enough.

Like when his dad would take him to the corner store for chips and a soda, but never ask how school was. Or when he'd let A.V. stay up late watching a movie, but fall asleep halfway through and snore so loud A.V. had to turn it off.

His affection, when it came, always felt like a mistake.

Like a man who forgot what he was supposed to do halfway through trying.

He never hit A.V.

He didn't have to.

His absence did more damage than his hands ever could.

His mom used to patch the silence with tired stories.

"Your daddy had it rough growing up," she'd say, lighting a cigarette with shaking fingers. "His own daddy used to beat him half to death. He don't know how to love right, but it don't mean he don't care."

A.V. wanted to believe that.

But when you're a kid, you don't measure love in excuses.

You measure it in presence.

In the way someone looks at you when you walk into a room.

In whether they show up when it's raining and you're stuck without a ride.

In whether they ask how you're really doing when your shoes are falling apart and you say, "I'm fine."

His father never asked.

So when the news came that night—Jace's cousin standing in the doorway, backlit by porchlight, voice tight with something between pity and warning—it didn't crack the world open.

It simply confirmed what A.V. already knew.

"He went off," the cousin said. "Your mom called the cops. Said he threw a chair at the wall. Cops showed up. Took him out in cuffs. Whole block saw it."

A.V. sat still on the carpet, arms around his knees.

The TV glowed blue across his face. The kung fu movie kept playing. A man on screen delivered a flying kick in slow motion, soundless.

"I'm good," A.V. said to Jace, voice flat.

"You sure?"

"Yeah."

He wasn't.

But it wasn't new.

There was no moment of collapse. No tears. No "why me?"

There was just silence.

And in that silence, A.V. knew two things.

One: He didn't have to pretend anymore. His father was gone, and it was finally okay to admit he'd never really been there.

Two: He'd been invisible in his own house for so long, it almost felt like freedom.

His mother didn't fall apart all at once.

She unraveled slowly, like a sweater losing its shape, one pulled thread at a time.

At first, it was little things. Skipping meals. Sleeping until noon. Forgetting what day it was. Burning eggs she used to make blindfolded. The ashtray stayed full. The sink stayed full. Her eyes, once sharp and full of fire, grew distant—like she was always looking through things instead of at them.

A.V. would come home from school and find her on the couch, curled under a blanket in the middle of the afternoon, reruns of old sitcoms playing too loud. Sometimes she'd talk at the screen. Sometimes she wouldn't talk at all.

He tried to help—kept his grades up, stayed out of trouble, fixed himself cereal for dinner when there was milk in the fridge. But nothing he did ever seemed to reach her. He started saying "I love you" just to see if she'd say it back.

Sometimes she did.

Most times she didn't.

By the time he was ten, she was using harder.

The pills in the orange bottles were no longer enough. Her purse started smelling like smoke and something sour. Strangers came and went. Men with tired eyes and dry laughs. One of them called A.V.

"little man" and tried to shake his hand like they were equals. He never came back.

He stopped inviting friends over. Stopped asking for lunch money. Stopped hoping for birthday candles.

He taught himself how to boil noodles, how to stretch a dollar store meal into two nights, how to sleep with his shoes on in case he had to leave in the middle of the night.

He learned how to be invisible in his own home.

Until the night Kristin showed up.

It was just past sunset. The apartment smelled like burnt plastic and sweat.

A.V. was on the floor, half-asleep on a rolled-up hoodie, listening to the same verse loop on his MP3 player, volume turned just loud enough to block out the shouting from the other room. A voice he didn't recognize. His mother's too. The clatter of something hitting the floor.

He didn't even flinch.

Then—three knocks on the door.

Sharp. Clean. Like someone wasn't there to ask questions.

He sat up.

The door opened before anyone answered it.

And there she was.

Kristin.

Framed in hallway light like a prophet who had lost all her patience.

Her lips were pursed. Her eyes scanned the room once, twice, and then she stepped inside like she'd been summoned.

"Get your things," she said.

A.V. didn't move.

His mother stumbled out from the bedroom, mascara streaked down her face, voice already defensive.

"Ma—he don't need—he's fine. We're fine."

Kristin didn't look at her.

"I said get your things."

There was no yelling. No pleading.

Just the sound of truth, spoken plainly.

A.V. stuffed what little he had into a grocery bag—two shirts, a notebook, a toothbrush with worn-down bristles. He didn't ask where they were going. He didn't say goodbye.

His mother didn't stop him.

She just sat down on the couch and lit another cigarette, hand trembling so hard she dropped the lighter twice.

As they left, Kristin put a folded envelope on the counter. Said nothing.

A.V. didn't look back.

Her house smelled like lemon balm and fabric softener and something warm in the oven.

The floors creaked like they were alive, but everything was clean. Every picture frame hung straight. There was a cross over the doorway and a row of hooks for coats.

No ashtrays. No strangers. No yelling.

That first night, she made him take a shower and brush his teeth. Gave him his own towel. A new toothbrush still in the package.

He didn't say much.

But when she turned off the light, and the room went quiet, he lay in bed and cried into the pillow like it was a secret.

The first week at Kristin's was weird in the way peace can be weird when you're used to chaos.

She had rules. Real ones. Taped to the fridge in bold marker.

1. Say what you mean.

2. Take your shoes off.

3. Don't lie, even when you're scared.

4. No yelling unless the house is on fire.

5. Everything in this home is ours—until you break it.

He read them over and over like scripture.

She woke up early every morning, before the sun, like she was still waiting on a world that forgot to call back. She played gospel on a little kitchen radio with a broken volume knob—it only had two settings: soft or judgment day.

She made oatmeal with cinnamon. Biscuits with honey. Beans and rice when she was tired.

She didn't hover.

Didn't smile much either.

But when she poured his coffee (half milk, always), she made sure to slide the sugar across the table without being asked.

She noticed when his socks had holes. Replaced them without comment. She asked once, gently, if he'd like to try sleeping with the light off. When he said no, she didn't press it.

And she never—not once—asked about his mother.

At school, he kept his head down.

The teachers didn't know what to do with him. He was smart, but never raised his hand. He finished work but left the answers blank. He got suspended once for punching a kid who threw a joke about "crack babies" across the hall like a frisbee. Didn't matter that he didn't start it.

Kristin didn't yell.

She picked him up, handed him a vanilla shake in the front seat, and said, "Next time, aim lower."

He laughed so hard he almost cried.

That night, he wrote his first real verse.

It started in pencil. In the margins of a vocabulary worksheet.

Just a few lines. Nothing special.

My daddy taught me nothing,
but silence still got weight.
So I speak in broken rhythms
just to ventilate the hate.

He didn't even know why it came out that way.

But it felt good.

He kept going.

By the end of the week, he had five pages—folded, wrinkled, scrawled in crooked lines like they were bleeding out of him. He hid them under his mattress, behind the heater, in the soles of old shoes. Not because he was ashamed.

Because they were sacred.

Kristin found one of the pages accidentally while doing laundry.

She didn't say much. Just looked at him from across the kitchen table one night and said, "If you're gonna write about pain, make sure you tell the truth. Not just yours. Other people's too."

Then she handed him a fresh notebook. No lines. Thick paper. Hard cover.

He stared at it like it was gold.

From that day on, he wrote every night.

Sometimes until the pen dried up. Sometimes just a few bars before sleep won the fight.

But he always wrote.

Because for the first time in his life, words felt like something that belonged to him.

Jace, Eli, and Tonio weren't blood.

But they knew A.V. better than most of his relatives ever tried to.

They met on the basketball court behind the school, on a day so hot the blacktop felt like it might crack open and swallow them whole. Jace had an old speaker in his backpack that barely worked, playing chopped-up beats and half-finished SoundCloud tracks. Eli always had Skittles in his pocket and a scab on his chin from fighting with his cousin. Tonio was the youngest, but the loudest. Always talking, always laughing, always ready to throw hands if someone said the wrong thing.

They weren't cool.

Not really.

They just *fit.*

Something about the way they all carried the same invisible weight. You could see it in the way they watched doors, sat with their backs to walls, laughed too loud at stuff that wasn't funny just to keep the dark off.

A.V. didn't tell them about his mom. Or his dad. Or the nights at Kristin's when the words came too fast and too jagged for sleep.

He didn't have to.

They already knew.

Their bond got sealed on a cold November afternoon when A.V. got jumped by two eighth graders who said he was "acting too smart."

He came home with a split lip and a bruise blooming across his ribs.

The next day, Jace brought gloves.

Not boxing gloves. Winter gloves filled with quarters.

Eli didn't say a word—just handed A.V. a cherry Coke and stood next to him in the hallway like a silent warning.

Tonio skipped gym to scope out the lockers of the kids who did it.

Nothing ever came of it.

But from that day on, A.V. didn't walk home alone.

They weren't just loyal—they were **real**.

They made fun of his handwriting. Told him his early verses sounded like broken poetry and bad math. But when he got better—when the rhymes started hitting harder, when the metaphors had claws—they listened. For real.

"Say that one again," Jace would say. "Nah, go back—start at the top."

They started writing too. Sitting in the back of class, trading bars like baseball cards. Passing notebooks like sacred scripture. Freestyling on the corner until the sun dropped out of the sky.

"We ain't hard 'cause we wanna be,"
Tonio once spit, breathless.
"We hard 'cause the world pressed us flat
and we pushed back."

They were a crew.

Not a gang.

Not saints.

Just *boys trying to stay boys* in a place that rushed you into manhood like it was trying to win a bet.

Kristin called them "the loud ones."

But she never turned them away.

She kept extra frozen pizzas in the fridge and pretended not to hear them recording verses in the back room. She told A.V. once, "As long as they treat you right and close the damn door when they're yelling, they can stay."

That was her way of saying: *I see what they mean to you.*

It happened, years later, on a Friday.

One of those city-slick summer evenings where the sun didn't set so much as melt into the concrete. Sweat ran down backs like warnings. Kids ran barefoot through busted sprinklers. Mothers leaned out of second-floor windows, yelling names like spells.

A.V. was twenty-two. Out of school. Still local. Hoodie unzipped, eyes sharp, nerves bubbling under his skin like soda about to fizz over.

The courtyard behind Eli's apartment complex was packed—people milling around, lawn chairs and plastic cups in hand, old heads blasting Marvin Gaye next to teenagers arguing about who had the best drill album. Somebody was grilling something. The smell of charcoal and hot dogs twisted with weed smoke and the sweet rot of spilled Kool-Aid on pavement.

And there was a speaker.
Big. Rusted. Balanced on a milk crate like a throne.

A mic was getting passed around like contraband. Some kid named Ramir had been rapping for the last three minutes—mostly punch-lines, mostly loud.

People clapped. Not hard. But they clapped.

Then Tonio elbowed A.V. in the ribs.

"Yo. Go."

A.V. blinked. "Nah."

"Go."

"I didn't come to—"

"You always say that shit, and then you blow everyone's face off. Just go."

Before A.V. could argue, Jace grabbed the mic from Ramir mid-line—ignoring the stink-face—and held it out to A.V.

"Time for some real bars," he said.

A few people looked over. A couple laughed. A woman with curlers in her hair paused at her third-floor balcony, arms crossed.

A.V. took the mic with hands that didn't shake but sure as hell wanted to.

The beat hit first. Just a dusty loop—drums cracked and warbled like it had lived a life.

A.V. closed his eyes.
Breathed in through his nose.
Let the world melt.

And then—he started.
Not loud. Not angry. Just true.

"They say the streets don't love you,
but they raised me like a son—
fed me scraps and sermons,
baptized me in the sun..."

People stopped talking.

Someone near the speaker nodded slow.

He kept going.

"My pops dipped, my moms slipped—
got high and called it flight,
so I scribbled all my scars
until the verses came out right."

By the time he hit the third verse, kids had stopped playing. Grown men leaned against the brick walls like they were listening to the radio. Eli was bouncing like he'd caught the Holy Ghost. Even Ramir was nodding—grudgingly, but nodding.

And A.V.—he felt it.

That heat in the chest. That rising pulse. That impossible-to-fake moment where he wasn't just saying words.
He was heard.

And they clapped. This time, for real.

After, he handed the mic back and walked off like it was nothing. Sat on the curb, breathing heavy but trying not to smile too hard.

Tonio tossed a bottle of water at him.

"You killed that," he said. "I'm not even mad."

Eli grinned. "Bro, you had Ms. Williams up there fanning herself like she was in church."

A.V. just stared at the crowd, still scattered, still humming with energy.

He didn't say anything.

But in that moment, for the first time, he didn't feel small.

He didn't feel invisible.

He felt *seen.*

Word traveled slow and wide.

Not through flyers. Not through phone screens. Just *people talking.*

Someone's uncle said he heard a kid outside the complex spit a verse that made him feel like he'd just gone to church and therapy in the same breath. A girl from down the block recited one of his lines to her cousin the next morning on the bus. Ms. Williams—the one with the curlers—told her sister at the beauty shop that "a boy out here has something to say, and it ain't nonsense for once."

Nobody said his name.

Just "that kid."

"That verse."

"That night."

And somehow, A.V. knew.

Not because he wanted fame.

But because he started catching looks.

That slow, second kind of look. The *you got something in you* look.

He didn't say anything when it happened. Just nodded and kept moving. But inside?

Something lit.

He wrote with urgency now.

Not for approval. But to keep pace with the beat in his chest.

Bars would come to him in the shower, on the bus, while brushing his teeth. He kept a pen in every pocket, scraps of paper in his socks, his backpack, tucked behind the toilet tank.

"Pain got rhythm if you listen close.
That's why my notebook's full of ghosts."

He'd tape verses to the back of his door. Sometimes, when he was out, Kristin would find them.
She'd read them in silence, then put them back exactly where they were—but flattened, smoothed, like she was straightening something important.

It was her way of saying: *This matters.*

Eli started saying things like, "We gotta record you, man. People need to hear this."

Jace borrowed a busted USB mic from his cousin. They stacked pillows in the closet, taped foam to the walls, ran wires across the floor like tripwires for sound.

It sounded terrible.

But it felt *real.*

A.V. stood in that makeshift booth like it was the Apollo.

He spit into that mic with every cracked syllable, every ache, every line his father never said, every apology his mother couldn't make.

They burned CDs on the library computers. Passed them out hand to hand like secret gospel.

No streaming. No clout.

Just *presence.*

———— 🦋 ————

And that's how it started.

A voice.

A verse.

A neighborhood carrying the sound like smoke.

———— 🦋 ————

The first time Kristin heard one of his finished tracks, she didn't say a word.

She was in the kitchen, kneading dough for biscuits—elbows dusted in flour, gospel humming low in the background—when she heard his voice rise through the wall.

Not shouting.

Not playing.

Speaking.

The beat was shaky—homegrown, stitched together from borrowed software and a loop Jace pulled off YouTube. It clapped too hard in some places and dipped in others like it hadn't fully figured out how to stand.

But A.V.'s voice?

It cut through.

"Mama said don't look back,
but all my memories live in reverse.
Every blessing got a bruise,
and every rhyme got a hearse."

Kristin paused, hands in dough.

She closed her eyes.

Not because she needed to focus—because the sound went through her like something remembered. Like grief spoken in a new tongue.

She didn't knock. Didn't call out.

Just listened until the track ended.

Then she went back to kneading.

But softer.

And when A.V. came to the table later, fresh from the back room, she had his favorite mug waiting—hot tea, two sugars, no lecture.

Her way of saying: *That one landed.*

Something shifted after that.

Not overnight. Not loud.

Just—deeper.

A.V. started caring more about the words. Not just the rhyme, but the weight. Not just what sounded hard, but what felt true.

He rewrote verses three, four, five times. Cut whole bars if they didn't hit the way they needed to. Started reading Baldwin and Angelou and Nas like blueprints. Listening to voices that didn't just say things— but moved them.

He started recording with less heat, more precision.

He didn't just want to impress anymore.

He wanted to reach.

He wanted someone who'd never met him to feel like they had.

People noticed.

The older guys on the block stopped teasing and started nodding. A woman who used to complain about the noise turned to him one afternoon and said, "That last one… that was about your mama, wasn't it?"

He didn't answer.

She smiled anyway.

One evening, while folding laundry in the living room, Kristin said—without looking up—

"Your words are getting heavier."

A.V. froze. "That bad?"

"No," she said. "That honest."

He didn't respond.

Just went back to his room.

And wrote another sixteen.

He didn't know where he was going—only that he needed to walk.

The heat was starting to break, finally.
One of those afternoons where the sun backed off just enough to let the breeze talk.
Even the pavement seemed like it had nothing left to prove.

A.V. walked alone.

Hoodie on, notebook tucked under one arm, headphones around his neck playing a beat on loop—low, pulsing, like a heartbeat with too much to say.

The neighborhood felt different now.

Not better. Not worse. Just aware.

There was a woman sweeping her porch who paused, glanced at him, and nodded once like she knew a secret. A little boy on a bike rode past him, shouting, "Yo! You the kid who rapped at Eli's cook-out, right?"

A.V. just grinned and threw up a peace sign.

Around the corner, someone had tagged a wall with his initials— AV—sloppy and loud in red spray paint. Not his doing. He didn't even like it. But he left it there.

Let it breathe.

A man sitting on the stoop of a corner bodega lit a cigarette and looked him up and down.

"You the poet, huh?" he asked.

A.V. blinked. "I guess."

"Keep writing," the man said. "World needs it."

A.V. kept walking.

Didn't smile.

But something in his chest felt warmer.

Like maybe all the things he wrote in the dark were starting to flicker in the light.

He turned down the block toward Kristin's place—the steps he knew by sound, the windows that always caught the last bit of sunset.

As he reached the porch, he paused.

Closed his notebook.

Looked back.

The block didn't wave.

Didn't shout.

But it saw him.

And this time, he felt it.

He sat on the steps for a little while longer, notebook unopened on his lap, letting the evening settle into him.

The streetlights flickered on one by one like the city was slowly remembering its own name.

In the window behind him, the kitchen light glowed soft and steady. Smelled like greens and cornbread. Something warm. Something real.

Then the door cracked open.

Kristin's voice floated out, smooth and matter-of-fact, like it always did when she didn't want to make a big deal but wanted to make sure he heard her anyway.

"Dinner's hot, baby. Don't let it get cold."

A.V. didn't answer right away.

Just stood up, tucked the notebook under his arm, and stepped inside.

All the Time
We Had

Butterflies don't measure time in days. They measure it in
moments. And some moments stretch longer than a lifetime.

Y ears passed.

    Not in dramatic, cinematic fashion. No montage. No swelling
soundtrack.

Just days.

One after another.

The city kept spinning. The block changed—just enough to notice if
you paid attention. A new mural where an old liquor store used to be.
One less friend on the corner. A streetlight fixed. Another one broken.

A.V. had grown too.

He was twenty-six now.

No platinum plaques on the wall. No stadiums with his face ten stories high.

But the records were out. The shows were packed.

And his name buzzed from rooftops to barbershops like a secret everybody already knew.

Word spread the way it always had—quiet and true.

A kid who spit with fire.

Who didn't rap about chains or brands, but about things that made your bones ache.

Who told the truth raw—no costume, no apology.

YouTube videos passed phone to phone. Mixtapes burned and passed out in rolled-down windows. A small tour—three cities, two late payments, and one night where the crowd screamed his name so loud he forgot where he came from.

And Uziel?

He was seventeen.

Still the boy made of light—but taller now, broader in the shoulders, voice deeper.

A little more cautious.

A little more tired.

But still kind.

Still the one who helped carry groceries for a neighbor without being asked. Still the one who hugged his sister in the hall just because. Still the one who sat with the new kid at lunch before anyone else dared to.

The whole school knew him.

Not because he tried to be known.

But because being *good* makes an impression in a world that forgets how rare that is.

The day of the ceremony began like most good things do—quietly.

Sunlight filtered through the kitchen blinds in wide golden stripes. The kind that made everything feel softer. More possible. The kind of morning that makes you believe the world still knows how to be good.

Lena stood barefoot at the stove, flipping pancakes while humming something tuneless. Her hair was tied up, and she wore Brent's old academy sweatshirt over leggings—both sleeves dusted in flour. The radio played softly in the background. Uziel's name was printed neatly on a thick manila envelope sitting at the end of the counter.

Upstairs, Brent stood in the bathroom, suit pants on, shirt half-buttoned. He stared at himself in the mirror, jaw set, tie hanging around his neck like a question he wasn't ready to answer. He'd been quiet all week.

The kind of quiet that meant something was pulling at him from the inside.

Uziel was already dressed.

Dark gray slacks. A white dress shirt, sleeves rolled just once. His tie was slightly off-center, but that didn't matter. He wore it like he wore everything—with ease.

He moved through the house like he belonged in it. Like he carried the history of its walls in the way he opened the fridge or picked up his little sister's sneakers and set them by the door without saying a word.

He walked into the kitchen and kissed his mom on the cheek.

"You look handsome, baby," she said.

"You're just saying that 'cause I look like you."

"You wish," she laughed, flipping a pancake. "Sit down. Eat."

"I'm not nervous, you know."

"I didn't say you were."

"But if I was… this would be the perfect breakfast."

She smiled, and for a second, the room felt like it did years ago—when he was shorter, and mornings were cartoons and cereal and asking why the sun didn't have a bedtime.

Brent came down the stairs slowly, shoes polished, suit jacket slung over his arm.

He didn't say much—just nodded to his son, kissed Lena's temple, and poured himself a cup of coffee.

Uziel watched him carefully. Not suspicious—just... aware.

"Ready, old man?"

Brent gave a half-smile. "Always."

But his voice didn't quite match.

The car ride to the school was short.

Twelve minutes, maybe thirteen with the lights.

But it stretched.

Felt long in that way meaningful things do—like time itself was slowing down to take a better look.

Uzi sat in the back seat, earbuds in, not playing music. Just there to feel something familiar. He watched the world drift by outside the window—houses, hydrants, cracked sidewalks he used to ride his bike across. He could trace his life block by block.

Lena sat up front, holding the program in her lap. She didn't read it. Just held it.

Every so often, she glanced at Brent.

He hadn't said a word since they got in the car.

Hands at ten and two.

Eyes straight ahead.

Body? Present.

Mind? Elsewhere.

He was thinking about the speech. Not Uzi's. His.

What he might have to say if someone handed him a mic. If the principal asked him to stand up and share a few words about his son. About fatherhood. About legacy.

He rehearsed the phrases in his head.

"He's always been a good kid."

"He's the best of us."

"I'm just proud to be his dad."

They all felt rehearsed. Hollow. Like cardboard cutouts of things he wished he'd said more when it mattered.

And underneath it all?

There was that old itch.

That gnawing voice that whispered:
You're not really the reason he turned out like this.

You were gone too much.
You loved him, but you didn't always see him.

———— 🦋 ————

From the back seat, Uzi leaned forward a little.

"Dad?"

Brent blinked. "Yeah?"

"Did you lock the cruiser before we left the station?"

Brent laughed, exhaling sharply. "Yeah. I double-checked."

Uzi nodded. "You sure?"

"Triple-checked. You wanna go back and check again?"

"Maybe."

Lena smiled quietly and looked out her window.

———— 🦋 ————

The school came into view—big, square, brick-and-glass with a line of parked cars already forming along the curb.

Parents. Teachers. Proud chaos.

Brent pulled into a spot, turned off the engine, and sat there for a second longer than necessary.

Uzi opened the door.

"Let's do this," he said.

Not cocky.

Just steady.

Like he already knew what he was made of.

The car doors were open.
The breeze drifted through—soft and clean—carrying the scent of cut grass and that faint tang of spring: half dirt, half flowers, full of memory.

Uzi had stepped out already. He stood on the sidewalk, adjusting his tie in the reflection of the backseat window, smiling at his sister who was twirling in her dress, her laugh skipping like stones across the parking lot.

Brent hadn't moved yet.
He sat still, one hand resting on the wheel, the other gripping the program Lena had placed on the console before getting out.

His eyes weren't on the school.
They were on Uzi.

Watching the way he stood.
The way his shoulders held no weight they weren't meant to carry.
The way he moved like he didn't just belong in the world—he belonged to it.

Lena stood just outside the car now, leaning slightly into the open door, her body angled back toward Brent, one hand resting gently on the roof.

"You see him now, don't you?" she said—voice low, like speaking too loud might crack the moment.

Brent didn't look away.
He nodded once.
Then said, almost too quietly:

"He doesn't need me anymore."

Lena reached in and touched his hand—not to correct him, not to comfort him.
Just to hold him there, in the now.

"He always needed you," she said. "You just weren't always looking."

The words didn't hurt.
They didn't forgive either.
They just settled between them like truth.

Outside, Uzi looked back over his shoulder.
Grinned.

"You guys coming or what?"

Brent finally stepped out.
Closed the door behind him.
And walked toward his son.

The school auditorium smelled like floor polish, folding chairs, and something nostalgic—maybe construction paper and cheap perfume.

The lights were half-dimmed, warm and drowsy. Parents shifted in creaky rows, murmuring greetings and straightening programs. Teachers paced like stage managers. A few siblings sat swinging their feet, already half-bored and half-awake to something big.

Brent hadn't been in a school gym in years. Not like this. Not with a shirt tucked, tie neat, hands sweating slightly. He felt out of place in the best way. Like being invited to a moment he hadn't earned, but somehow needed to witness.

He held Lena's hand without thinking.

She held it back like she always had.

Uziel sat backstage with a group of other honorees, all dressed up in their various versions of "best." Some squirmed. Some whispered. He sat still, calm. A paper folded in his pocket. A speech, maybe. Maybe not.

When they called his name, the sound seemed to *pause* the room—not from surprise, but from recognition.

People clapped.

Some stood.

One teacher wiped her eye before she even knew she was crying.

Brent watched him take the stage.

Shoulders back. Eyes forward. Tie slightly off-center. That same ease he wore like a birthright.

He didn't look nervous.

He looked *ready.*

The applause faded.

The microphone waited.

Uziel stepped up.

No paper. No notes.

He smiled, slow and genuine.

"Thanks," he said. "I didn't really plan to talk long. But I guess if you're up here, you're supposed to say something."

Soft laughter. Lena squeezed Brent's hand.

Uziel paused, let the silence breathe.

"I've had a good life," he said. "I know that's weird to say at seventeen. But it's true. Not because everything's been easy, but because I've had love. And I've had people who saw me."

He looked toward the crowd.

Eyes found his dad. Then his mom.

Then his sister—who waved like she didn't care about ceremony at all.

"I think seeing someone is the most powerful thing you can do," Uziel continued. "And I just hope I've made other people feel seen the way people have done that for me."

There was a beat of stillness.

Then he grinned.

"And also... I hope my little sister stops stealing my socks."

Laughter again. Real this time. The kind that ripples.

Uziel nodded to the crowd. "Thank you."

And that was it.

No crescendo. No tears.

Just *truth*.

When he stepped off stage, the applause kept going.

Not because he said something perfect.

But because he said something *true*.

After the ceremony, the hallway outside the auditorium buzzed with bodies and voices—parents congratulating one another, teachers trying to keep their clipboards from getting stepped on, kids half-undoing their ties and pretending they didn't care they were proud.

Lena held Uziel's award close to her chest like it was something living.

Brent stood nearby, unsure of where to place his hands.

Their daughter kept tugging at Uzi's jacket sleeve, asking if she could wear his "fancy medal thing."

Uzi just laughed and let her.

That's when people started approaching.

The first was Mrs. Raymond from the front office.

Petite. Always smelled like peppermint and strong coffee.

"I just wanted to say," she said, looking directly at Brent and Lena, "your boy is… something else. The way he helps the younger students? That doesn't show up on any report. But we see it."

Lena smiled. "Thank you."

Brent nodded. "Appreciate that."

Then came Mr. Danielson, the math teacher with a permanent squint and an armful of folders.

"I've been teaching for twenty-five years," he said. "And I've had a lot of smart kids. But your son? He listens in a way most don't. He makes other students better just by being next to them."

Brent didn't quite know how to respond.

So he just said, "He gets that from his mom."

Lena didn't correct him.

She just slipped her hand into his.

There was a girl's mother too—someone Brent didn't recognize.

She had a kind face and tired eyes, and she held her daughter close like she was afraid to let go.

"My daughter had a really hard time this year," she said quietly. "Didn't want to come to school anymore. Then she started sitting next to your son at lunch."

She looked at Uziel, then back to Brent and Lena.

"He didn't fix everything. But she smiled again. That mattered."

It kept coming.

A counselor who said he volunteered to help organize lockers.

A janitor who said he never left trash behind, not once.

A kid in a hoodie who shyly asked if he could take a picture with Uzi before his parents made them leave.

Uzi took the photo.

No big smile. Just the calm, steady look of someone **who had given something quietly and gotten love in return.**

When they finally left, the sky had turned a pale gold.

Everything felt *soft*. Unfolded.

Brent walked a little behind them—Lena and the kids in front, laughing, the medal clinking softly against Uzi's chest with every step.

He watched them in silence.

And for the first time in a long while, he wasn't thinking about himself.

He was thinking about *them*.

That night, long after dinner had been cleaned up and the house had settled into its usual soft quiet, Uziel sat on the edge of his bed, still in his ceremony clothes.

The medal lay on his desk, turned slightly so the light caught it just right. His tie hung on the doorknob. The program was folded neatly in his backpack.

The room smelled faintly of the cologne Lena had spritzed on him that morning—like citrus and something clean, something lifted.

He stared at the ceiling for a while.
Then he stood up.

Went to his desk.

Opened the drawer.

Pulled out his sketchpad.

It was worn around the edges, corners curled from being stuffed in bags and beneath pillows. He flipped past the early pages—super-heroes in capes, stick-figure comics, wild action scenes with sharp speech bubbles and too many exclamation points.

Then came the newer ones.

More thoughtful.

More *possible*.

A sketch of his school. A drawing of his little sister saving a cat from a tree. A comic where the villain wasn't evil—just lonely.

And finally, a blank page.

He picked up a pen and started something new.

He didn't know what it would become.

But he knew he wasn't done.

The medal was cool.

The applause was nice.

But there was still more to do.

Still more to give.

Still more to become.

The house was warm that night.

Not just from the dinner Lena had made, or the soft hum of the dishwasher working through the last of the dishes—but from the kind of peace that settles in after a day well lived.

Brent had changed into a T-shirt. Lena wore one of his sweatshirts. Their daughter was curled on the couch, half-watching a movie she'd seen thirteen times already. Uziel had disappeared into his room with his sketchpad and a quiet smile that hadn't left since the stage lights hit him.

It should've been the end of the day.

But then Lena said it—soft, playful, out of nowhere.

"We should go out."

Brent looked up from the chair. "Out?"

"Yeah. Celebrate. One more scoop before we call it a night."

He blinked. "Ice cream?"

"Why not?" she shrugged. "He deserves it. We all do."

From the hallway:

"Chocolate chip cookie dough or I'm not going."

His sister perked up, already reaching for her shoes.

"Can I get sprinkles?"

Brent sighed, dramatic.

"Alright. But if they don't have rocky road, I'm driving us to the next county."

Lena grinned.

Uziel grabbed his golden hoodie.

And just like that, they were in the car.

No big decision. No plan.

Just a moment.

The kind that passes through time like a whisper, only to echo forever.

The Wrong Side of a Green Light

A butterfly has no concept of consequence. It moves through
the world with lightness, never knowing which wingbeat
shifts the wind—and which one starts the storm.

Two shadows crept into a black Buick as it idled at the edge of
the block.

The car didn't roar to life—it *crawled*. Slow. Measured. Like it was
trying not to wake the night.

The street barely noticed.

There were too many distractions.

A basketball echoed on cracked pavement two blocks over. A grill
hissed somewhere close, smoke curling into the powerlines. Music
drifted from an open window. Kids yelled at each other in the kind of
play that sometimes turned.

And the Buick moved.

Low and steady.

Inside, the cabin was thick with heat and silence.

It smelled like sweat, smoke, and something sour—like metal left out in the rain.

Neither shadow spoke.

One pulled his hoodie tighter. The other adjusted something beneath his seat.

They didn't need to talk. Not anymore.

Whatever they were about to do had already been decided.

The city just didn't know it yet.

The Buick rolled through a yellow light like it didn't care if it made it or not.

The glow washed across the hood, gold bleeding into black, then gone.

The men inside didn't flinch.

Didn't blink.

The driver tapped the wheel with one finger—slow, off-beat. The passenger pulled the hood farther over his face, eyes fixed on the middle distance.

Not focused.

Not blank.

Just waiting.

They passed two teenagers sitting on the curb, sharing a bag of chips. The boys watched the car with half-interest, half-instinct. Their eyes followed it long after it passed.

———— ❦ ————

The Buick didn't stop.

Didn't speed up either.

———— ❦ ————

The streets narrowed.

The rhythm changed.

Fewer porches. More fences. The light poles flickered, not in protest—just fatigue. A mural on the side of a liquor store blurred past the window: a boy with angel wings holding a violin. Someone had tagged over the wings in red paint.

The music in the car was still playing—barely audible. Something dark and mean. More pulse than melody.

The driver looked down at the phone once.

No texts.

Just the time.

Then he killed the music.

Silence came down like a lid.

———— 🦋 ————

One of them reached beneath the seat.

Fingers found something long, cold, metallic.

He didn't pull it out.

Just held it.

The weight was familiar.

The car turned right.

Then another right.

Now they were circling.

Like wolves.

Or something slower.

Something *inevitable*.

———— 🦋 ————

The Buick slid past its third intersection in twelve minutes.

Still no words.

Still no rush.

Just the low hum of tires and heat.

Inside, the driver adjusted the rearview again—second time in less than a block. He wasn't checking for cops. He was checking *himself.*

And what he saw?

Didn't blink.

Didn't flinch.

Just stared back.

The passenger rested one hand on the window frame, the other still draped casually over something heavy in his lap. No twitch. No tension.

But the silence between them had shifted.

It was no longer quiet.

It was *ready.*

———— 🦋 ————

The blocks began to look familiar now.

The light poles. The way the corners opened. The curve of the street leading up to the intersection.

One of them pointed, slow and deliberate.

The driver nodded.

They didn't speak.

They didn't need to.

———— 🦋 ————

The car turned left, easing down the lane like it belonged there. It crept past a shuttered corner store, past a closed barbershop with flyers still flapping in the night wind.

Then they saw it.

The figure.

Not clear.

Not even confirmed.

Just *there*.

A shape near the curb at the far end of the intersection.

Wrong place.

Wrong time.

Wrong life.

———— 🦋 ————

Inside the Buick, the silence cracked—just a little.

A deep inhale.

A safety clicked.

A thought that didn't turn back.

The light ahead turned green.

Brent didn't speed.

Didn't hesitate either.

He eased the car forward like any father would—with his wife in the passenger seat, one kid asleep in the back, and another watching the world like it still deserved his attention.

Uziel leaned slightly into the window, the cool night air running along his cheek, his fingers tapping softly to a rhythm he wasn't fully aware of.

They were close now.

Two more blocks to the ice cream shop.

Brent glanced at the clock on the dash.

9:47 PM.

In the passenger seat, Lena flipped down the visor to check her reflection. Smiled to herself. Reached over and squeezed Brent's hand without a word.

He squeezed back.

That one small, unspoken moment said everything.

Said: *This was a good day.*

Said: *I'm glad we're here.*

Said: *We're still us.*

———— 🦋 ————

Behind them, their daughter stirred, yawned, and shifted beneath her hoodie.

Uziel turned slightly.

"You alright?"

She nodded, still half-asleep.

He smiled.

That same smile that made teachers soften, friends feel safe, strangers wave back.

And then—

———— 🦋 ————

The headlights caught the corner.

And the black Buick—

was already there.

———— 🦋 ————

It wasn't like they say in the movies.

There was no slow motion.

No time-stretched scream.

No swelling music.

It happened fast.

Too fast.

The Buick rolled up.

The window dropped.

And the flash came first—

a burst of light.
then noise.
then glass.

A popping sound—softer than expected.

Like fireworks too close.

Then tires squealed.

Rubber screamed on pavement.

And just like that—

it was over.

———— 🦋 ————

Brent's ears were ringing.

He couldn't hear Lena's voice—only see her mouth moving, wide and full of something primal.

His foot slammed the brake.

The car swerved to a stop.

The back window was gone.

Gone.

Shattered.

His daughter screamed—sharp and animal.

He turned in his seat—

And **Uziel wasn't moving.**

Somewhere, as the Buick disappeared into the blur of red taillights and panic, a car stereo blasted out into the night.

A track Brent didn't recognize—
but Lena did.

A.V.'s voice, low and raw, bleeding from someone's speakers.

"We survivors, we sinners, we saints in the same skin—
born with fire in our mouths and nowhere to spit it."

The line looped.

Then faded into the dark.

Brent couldn't move.

Not at first.

His hands were on the wheel.
Then on the door.
Then on nothing.

His brain screamed *go*, but his body was stuck in some other language.

He heard a voice—his daughter's.
High. Panicked.
"He's not okay! He's not okay! Daddy, is he okay?!"

He turned around.

And **Lena was already out of the car.**

Door wide.

Her knees on the pavement.

Cradling Uziel's head in her lap, her body rocking in tight, desperate waves.

She wasn't trying to stop the bleeding.

She wasn't trying to calm him.

She was just holding him.

As if maybe if she held hard enough, he'd come back into her arms from wherever he was drifting.

Brent stumbled out.

The night was loud now.

Not with gunfire.

But with **everything else.**

A man ran from his porch. "Call 911!"

A woman down the block screamed.

Another person filmed.

Of course they filmed.

But Brent couldn't hear them.

He couldn't hear anything but that *ringing.*

High and endless.

Like a bell that only sounded when the world was ending.

He dropped to his knees.

Hands hovering over Lena's shoulder, over Uzi's chest, not knowing where to touch, how to help, *how to fix it.*

There was **so much blood.**

Too much.

———— 🦋 ————

Lena's voice cracked open.

"No no no—please God—*please—Uzi—baby—Uzi—breathe for me—breathe—*"

But he wasn't breathing.

Not like he should've been.

Not like **before.**

———— 🦋 ————

When the sirens came, Brent didn't rise to meet them.

He didn't wave.

He didn't shout.

He just sat there, knees on asphalt, watching the red and blue lights dance across the windshield.

And for the first time in his life—

He truly believed he'd failed.

———— 🦋 ————

The ride to the hospital felt like it happened underwater.

The sirens wailed, but Brent couldn't tell if they were behind them or inside his own skull.

Lena rode in the back of the ambulance, her hands slick with blood, her voice cracked down to a whisper. She never let go of Uziel's hand—not even when the medics told her to clear the way. She pressed her forehead to his and begged him to hold on.

"Please, baby. Please just stay."

Brent followed in his car.

He drove in silence.

Didn't speak.

Didn't blink.

Didn't pray.

He just gripped the wheel like it might hold him together.

The ER doors hissed open.
Fluorescent lights. The sting of antiseptic.
Voices.
Too many.

"Male, seventeen, GSW to the back—entry right shoulder blade, no exit wound—"
"BP crashing—"
"Get him into Trauma 2—now!"

Lena tried to follow.
They held her back.
She screamed—not words, just sound.

Brent stepped in, wrapped his arms around her from behind, and she collapsed into him like her bones had finally given up.

He didn't cry.
Not yet.
He just held her.
Tight.
Like if he let go, she might disappear too.

———— 🦋 ————

They waited in a room with mint-green walls and broken magazines.

Their daughter curled up in a chair, asleep, one hand still clutched around the corner of her brother's program from the ceremony.

Lena rocked in place.

Muttering his name over and over like it was a spell.

Brent sat perfectly still.

Except for his right leg.

It wouldn't stop shaking.

———— 🦋 ————

A nurse walked in, but she didn't speak.

Her face said enough.

Behind her, a doctor followed—older, calm, *used to this.*

But this wasn't *anyone.*

This was **Uziel.**

Brent stood up, but Lena was already halfway across the room.

The doctor opened his mouth—

But Brent already knew.

He didn't need to hear it.

He could see it in Lena's knees—how they gave out.

How she screamed like the sky was falling.

How the nurse caught her just before she hit the floor.

———— 🦋 ————

He didn't remember what the doctor said.

Only the phrase that stayed etched in his mind:

"He didn't suffer long."

As if that made it better.

As if that brought him back.

———— 🦋 ————

And just like that,

the brightest thing in their world

was gone.

———— 🦋 ————

Outside the hospital, the air had cooled.

Not cold.

Just *hollow.*

The kind of air that doesn't carry sound the same way anymore.

Brent stood alone by the parking lot.

Didn't smoke.

Didn't cry.

Just stood there.

One hand on his car.

One hand hanging.

His fingers were still stained red.

———— 🦋 ————

Brent stared up at the sky.

No stars.

Too many streetlights.

Too much noise.

He wanted to scream.
He wanted to run.
He wanted to pray.
He wanted to *die*.

But he didn't move.

He just stood there.

Until the motion-sensor light above the ambulance bay flicked off.

And everything went dark.

The Echo That Stays

Some butterflies don't live long. But when they pass through,
even the trees lean in to feel them.

T he sunlight poured into Uziel's room like it always had—soft,
golden, warm.

It landed on the crumpled bedsheets, the scuffed sneakers by the door,
the sketchbook still open on his desk. A half-finished drawing waited
patiently—lines shaped into something gentle, something unfinished.

The medal from the ceremony still hung on the bedpost.

No one had touched it.

No one had touched anything.

The room was too quiet.

Not peaceful.

Just wrong.

Like a song that ended mid-chorus and never came back.

On Westlake Avenue, a row of chalk drawings lined the sidewalk in front of the school.

Some were messy. Some barely legible. But all of them said his name.

"Uzi forever."
"You were light."
"Thank you."

One was a drawing of Spider-Man—arms out, mid-swing, a gold medal around his neck.

The kids had started it that morning, passing the chalk from one to another, nobody saying much. Just drawing. Heads low. Knees scraped. Colors blurring together where their hands trembled.

No one was told to. No teacher assigned it.

They just *did* it.

Because grief finds a way.

At Tony's Diner, the usual breakfast rush came and went.

People ordered pancakes. Eggs. Hash browns.

No one ate quickly.

The waitstaff moved slower. No one complained.

Tony poured free coffee refills like he didn't notice he was doing it.

And every time the bell above the door jingled, he looked up—not expecting Uziel, but still hoping to hear him shout something dumb like *"I'm back for round two, Tony!"*

At the end of the counter, a napkin sat untouched with **"Sunshine special"** written on it in black ink.

Tony left it there all day.

Didn't explain it.

Didn't need to.

Near the park, the mural wall had been painted over.

Fresh blue background.

Blank canvas.

The artists hadn't started yet.

They stood around in silence, nodding, holding spray cans like microphones they weren't ready to speak into.

Someone said, "We should put him up there."

Another replied, "He already is."

Back at the bodega, the clerk lit another candle.

Set it beside the first.

Then went back to restocking shelves, eyes red, jaw tight.

When a little boy came in to buy candy, the clerk pointed at the candles and said softly:

"He used to stand right where you're standing."

The boy nodded, wide-eyed.

Left without buying anything.

The city didn't stop.

But it walked slower that day.

It looked up more often.

And when it did—

It looked for **him.**

The house hadn't changed.

Not really.

The same coats hung by the door. The same cereal box sat half-folded in the pantry. A drawing Uziel made when he was eight still hung on the fridge, colors faded and corners curled.

But the silence?

It was different now.

It wasn't the kind that came from rest.

It was the kind that *lingered*. That *watched*. That *waited* to be broken.

And no one wanted to be the first to break it.

———— ❦ ————

Brent sat at the kitchen table with a blank piece of paper in front of him.

It wasn't for notes.

It wasn't a letter.

It was just *there*.

His hands were clasped. His jaw clenched. His eyes kept finding things he hadn't seen in years—the chipped corner of the counter, the water ring from Uzi's favorite mug.

He didn't speak.

Didn't blink much either.

Across the table, Lena hadn't moved in ten minutes.

She sat with her hands in her lap, staring at the floor.

She looked like someone trying not to fall through it.

Their daughter lay curled on the couch, knees to chest, wrapped in one of Uzi's sweatshirts. She hadn't said a word since they got home.

She clutched one of his drawings like a stuffed animal—creases deep, corners soft, her thumb brushing it in steady circles.

In Uzi's room, the sun had shifted.

The light now hit the sketchbook dead center.

Pages fluttered from the fan in the hallway.

No one closed the door.

They couldn't bring themselves to.

It felt too final.

Too much like *goodbye.*

The silence cracked around dinner time.

No one had eaten.

The kitchen smelled faintly of what was left from the night before— garlic, pepper, something sweet that had gone untouched.

Lena was still sitting at the table, her palms pressed flat against her thighs, like she didn't trust herself to move.

Brent stood by the sink, staring into an empty glass like it might explain something to him.

And then—

She said it.

Not loud.

Not broken.

Just… truth.

"He's not coming home."

Her voice didn't shake.

That was the worst part.

It was flat. Final.

A period, not a question.

Brent turned to face her.

"I know," he said.

His mouth opened again like he wanted to say more.

But nothing came.

Not yet.

She looked up at him, eyes swollen, dry now. Too dry.

"I keep thinking he's gonna walk in. Every time I hear the floor creak."

Brent walked over, pulled out the chair across from her, sat down slow.

"The house feels too big."

Lena nodded.

"So does the world."

They sat like that for a long time.

No more words.

Just a kind of breathing that hurt to listen to.

In the other room, their daughter sat cross-legged on the floor beside the couch.

The sweatshirt she'd worn all day was bunched in her lap.

She had Uzi's old sketchbook open, her little fingers tracing the lines of a superhero he never finished—cape only half-drawn, one boot missing.

She didn't cry.

She didn't speak.

She just traced.

Over and over.

Then, quietly, she whispered:

"He's still in here."

And kept tracing.

Like she was keeping him warm.

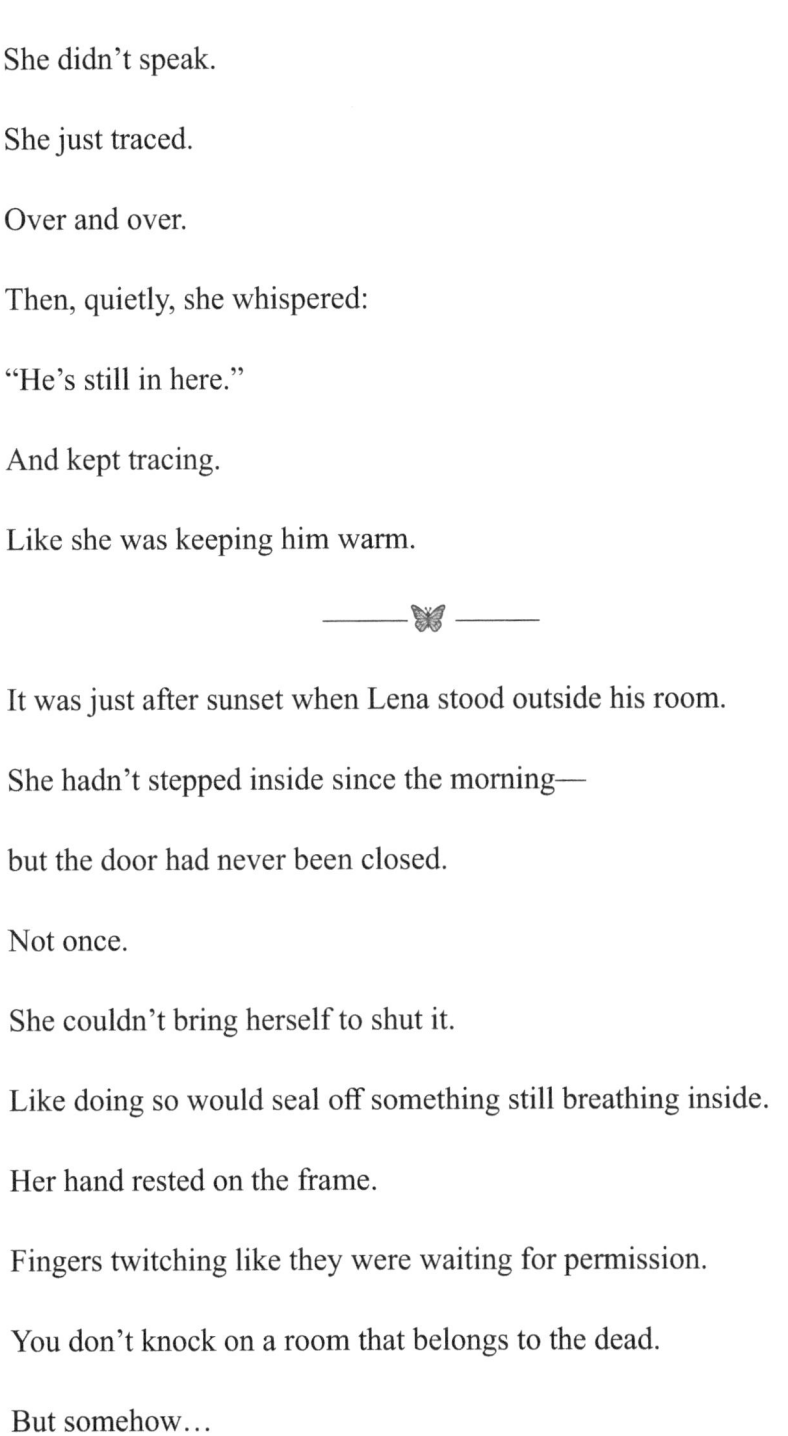

It was just after sunset when Lena stood outside his room.

She hadn't stepped inside since the morning—

but the door had never been closed.

Not once.

She couldn't bring herself to shut it.

Like doing so would seal off something still breathing inside.

Her hand rested on the frame.

Fingers twitching like they were waiting for permission.

You don't knock on a room that belongs to the dead.

But somehow…

you still pause before crossing the threshold.

The hallway behind her was dark.

The rest of the house had gone still again.

She stepped inside, slow.

Quiet.

Like he might still be there—

just out of sight.

The air inside hit her like a memory.

It smelled like shampoo and old pencils.

Like detergent and something warm.

Like *him.*

Lena stepped in slow, arms crossed, holding herself tighter than she meant to.

The sun was gone now, but the last traces of light clung to the walls like they didn't want to leave.

She looked at everything—

The bed, unmade.

The sketchbook, still open.

The crumpled hoodie in the corner.

The drawings on the wall. The ones she used to pretend annoyed her, but secretly loved.

His desk chair was turned out, like he'd just gotten up.

There was a sock on the floor.

And a gum wrapper on the nightstand.

She didn't touch anything.

Not yet.

She sat on the edge of the bed like she was waiting for someone.

Her hands went to her lap.

And slowly, gently, she picked up the medal.

Held it in both palms.

Stared at it like it could explain something.

————— 🦋 —————

"You were so good," she whispered.

"You were so good."

Her voice cracked then.

Just once.

She didn't sob.

Didn't collapse.

She just bowed her head, as if in prayer, and let the silence wrap around her like arms.

She stayed there until the light was gone completely.

Until the room was just shapes.

And her breathing was the only sound.

Echoes in
the Chorus

A butterfly doesn't get to choose where the wind takes it. But
it always leaves a pattern in the air behind.

The music was loud enough to shake the floorboards.

A.V. stood in the corner of the living room, half-finished drink
in one hand, his other tucked into the pocket of a jacket he hadn't
taken off yet. The party was spilling over with people—industry kids,
friends of friends, people who smiled too fast and complimented his
lyrics with the wrong lines.

He nodded when people came up to him.

Dapped up strangers he didn't remember meeting.

Smiled politely when they asked about the next album.

He wasn't *unhappy*.

He was just **tired**.

Every room he walked into these days felt like a stage.

And sometimes, he didn't want to perform.

Across the room, someone was flipping through TV channels with the volume too low to hear.

The music drowned it out—bass-heavy and careless.

But A.V. caught something out of the corner of his eye.

A news crawl.

"17-year-old killed in random shooting..."

He blinked.

Didn't read the rest.

Then someone turned the volume up—for the TV, not the music.

"—was returning home with his family after attending a school awards ceremony earlier that night. His name was Uziel Brooks. He was a beloved student, athlete, and artist—"

The screen showed a school photo.

Bright eyes. Tie crooked. Smile so wide it barely fit the frame.

A.V. froze.

The drink in his hand suddenly felt heavier.

He walked toward the screen.

Someone tried to talk to him on the way—he didn't hear.

The voiceover continued:

"—his father, Brent Brooks, a decorated police officer in the 9th district, was driving the car when the shots were fired…"

Brent.

Brent.

That name hit harder than the headline.

Harder than the photo.

Harder than the gunshots in the story.

He knew that name.

Not from news.

Not from music.

From a night he didn't talk about.

A ledge.

A storm.

A voice that had pulled him back.

"You're loved. Not just by your people—but by *every* good heart in this world."

A.V. sat down on the armrest of the nearest couch, slow.

He rubbed his jaw.

Eyes locked on the screen.

And when the segment ended—when the photo disappeared—

He still saw it.

He saw Brent's face.

Saw the kid's smile.

And then he remembered the line.

The line that had just been playing in the song before the segment started.

"Born with fire in our mouths and nowhere to spit it."

And suddenly, he didn't want to perform anymore.

A.V. didn't move.

The party kept going around him like nothing had happened.

People laughed. Someone dropped a bottle. The music skipped. Someone else shouted, "Run that back!" and pointed toward the speaker with a red Solo cup like it was the only thing that mattered.

But A.V. couldn't hear any of it.

All he could hear was the **line**.

That damn line.

"He was a beloved student… an artist…"

He pressed a hand to his chest like something inside was pulling tight from the inside.

Not pain.

Not yet.

Just *weight*.

He tried to remember the last thing he'd written.

Something hard. Sharp. Full of bars about broken homes and bleeding blocks. Another verse about how no one makes it out.

People ate that shit up.

But now?

It sounded hollow.

He was making pain sound beautiful.

And someone had died while his words played in the background.

Maybe not from his music.

But **through it.**

Through the world it came from.

The one he hadn't left behind, not really.

The one he still painted in verse—*grimy, brutal, real.*

———— 🦋 ————

He stood slowly.

Moved toward the kitchen like he meant to get another drink.

Didn't.

Just leaned against the counter, knuckles white.

Somebody tried to dap him up. "Yo, that line about the angel with a bloody halo? *Hard.*"

A.V. nodded without looking.

"Yeah."

Then, softer:

"Too hard."

He pulled his phone from his jacket.

Opened Instagram.

Typed "Uziel Brooks."

Found the school photo again.

And then—

there it was.

Another post.

A news image.

A different photo.

Grainier.

Older.

Brent.

Younger. In uniform. Smiling next to a police cruiser.

A.V. knew that face.

Even before the badge.

Even before the station.

"You don't get to give up, son.
Not tonight.
You matter too much."

———— 🦋 ————

The phone trembled in his hand.

He didn't know if it was him or the air.

But for the first time in years,

A.V. felt **ashamed of his voice.**

Not because it wasn't true.

But because it hadn't been *enough*.

———— 🦋 ————

He moved through the crowd like he wasn't there.

People kept trying to pull him back in.

"Yo, A.V., you dipping already?"
"Bro, we still need you for the freestyle!"
"You good?"

He didn't answer.

Didn't stop.

Just nodded.

That same industry nod. The one that says *yeah, yeah, later*, even when there's no later coming.

———— 🦋 ————

The front door opened and the night slapped him in the face.

Cool air. Real air.

No bass. No clinking glasses. No autotune.

Just traffic. Sirens in the distance.
A city that didn't know who he was—and didn't care.

He pulled his hoodie up.

Walked down the stairs.

Didn't call a ride.

Didn't check his phone.

He just **walked**.

No destination.

No direction.

Just *away.*

———— 🦋 ————

With every step, pieces of the night unraveled behind him.

The kid's face.

The name.

The father.

The song.

The image of Brent in his memory.

Hands outstretched on a rooftop. Voice calm, even in the rain.

Telling him **he mattered**.

And now?

Brent had lost the one person that mattered most.

———— 🦋 ————

A.V. shoved his hands deep into his pockets.

He couldn't write this.

Not tonight.

Not yet.

There weren't enough bars in the world for this kind of silence.

———— 🦋 ————

The pavement was cracked beneath his sneakers.

Each step felt louder than it should have, like the city wanted him to hear it breaking too.

A.V. kept his head down, hoodie up, shoulders hunched—not because he was hiding, but because *he couldn't carry this upright yet.*

He passed closed storefronts.

A barber pole still spinning even though the shop had long gone dark.

A mural half-finished on a brick wall—spray cans scattered at its base, waiting for tomorrow.

He passed a stoop where two old men played dominoes most nights. Tonight, it was empty. Just a folding chair and a soda can dented at the lip.

Everything looked the same.

But nothing felt right.

He cut down a block he hadn't walked in a while.

The one near the old corner store where Kristin used to send him for bread and eggs.

He stopped outside the metal gate.

The sign was gone. The windows boarded.

He remembered the first verse he ever wrote—right there on the curb.

A line about survival.

A line about fire.

He said it out loud once, years ago, and a man leaning on the mailbox told him he had something.

"Don't waste that fire, boy," he'd said.

A.V. thought about that now.

All these years later.

That fire had moved people.

Lit stages.

Lit *souls*.

But it had also cast shadows.

He kept walking.

Past the bus stop with the broken bench.

Past the alley where he and Jace used to freestyle after school, spitting rhymes at brick walls like they owed him something.

The wind picked up.

He pulled the hoodie tighter, tucked his chin.

He wasn't cold.

He just felt **empty.**

Like his voice had gone somewhere ahead of him and didn't wait for him to catch up.

———— 🦋 ————

Then he reached it.

The old building.

Abandoned now.

Still standing.

Still tall.

The one with the rooftop.

The ledge.

The rain.

The boy.

The cop.

The turning point.

———— 🦋 ————

He stared up at it for a long time.

Didn't move.

Didn't blink.

Just stood there,

listening for something that wasn't coming.

———— 🦋 ————

He stood there.

Hands buried in his pockets.

Hood low.

Eyes locked on that rooftop.

It looked smaller now.

Less mythic. Less terrifying.

Just bricks and ledges and old steel that had weathered storms he didn't even remember.

But he remembered **that night**.

The wet sound of rain hitting concrete.

The thunder behind his heartbeat.

The way the wind pushed his hoodie back like it was trying to keep him from jumping.

And **Brent.**

Soaked through.

Breathing heavy.

Voice calm.

"You matter, son."
"You're not done yet."
"There's love for you—more than you know."

A.V. had never told anyone that story.

Not really.

Only pieces.

Only lines tucked between metaphors and hooks.

He didn't want pity.

He didn't want applause.

He just... *wanted it to mean something.*

And now?

Now that man had lost his son.

Because of a bullet.
Because of a night.

Because of music A.V. hadn't made to hurt, but that had somehow become the background noise to a tragedy.

He didn't even know at first.
Not until the news cam on at the party.
Someone had turned the volume
up—just enough to catch the reporter's voice over the noise.

Live on the scene.

Interviewing a woman who'd heard the shots.

But behind her—off to the edge of the frame—there were a few guys mugging for the camera.

Laughing.

Throwing signs.

One of them dancing like it was all a joke.

And that's when he heard it.

Not the gunfire. Not the screaming.

The music.

His track.

Playing from a car parked just out of frame.

Nobody else at the party seemed to notice.

But A.V. did.

He heard it clear.

And it gutted him.

He sat down on the curb.

Didn't speak.

Didn't cry.

He just *watched* the place where his life had been saved.

And wondered how the hell he was supposed to live with the fact that someone else's hadn't been.

The front door clicked open like it was trying not to wake anyone.

Brent stepped onto the porch, still in yesterday's clothes. Still wearing the creases of a man who hadn't slept, hadn't eaten, hadn't *exhaled*.

The air outside was cooler than he expected.

That spring kind of cool—damp at the edges.
Smelled like cut grass. Wet concrete. And something burnt in the distance.

The street was still.

Too still.

A bird chirped from the power line.

He hated it for sounding so normal.

He sat on the porch steps.

Not with purpose.

Just because his legs didn't want to hold him anymore.

His hands hung between his knees.

Calloused palms. Dry knuckles.
Hands that had carried so much—
but not enough.

Not when it mattered.

———— 🦋 ————

Across the street, a neighbor waved.
He didn't wave back.

She looked like she might come over.

He looked away until she changed her mind.

———— 🦋 ————

He used to sit out here with Uzi.

Late nights. Hot cocoa. Cheap lawn chairs.

They'd watch lightning bugs float in the dark.

Talk about Spider-Man.

Talk about college.

Talk about nothing at all.

And now?

Now he just sat there.

With the weight of everything **he didn't say.**

The porch creaked beneath him as he shifted, slowly, hands rubbing his knees like maybe if he scrubbed hard enough, he could erase what they hadn't done.

He didn't hear the door open behind him.

Didn't hear the footsteps, either.

Just felt the weight of **his phone** being placed beside him on the step.

Lena had left it.

No words.

Just the phone.

And the message it carried.

The screen was lit with a name he didn't know.

But the text was simple.

"I think this is meant for you. Listen all the way through."

An audio clip.

Thirty seconds.

Brent hesitated.

Then tapped play.

A beat kicked in.

Not loud. Not flashy.

Just steady.

Measured.

Then A.V.'s voice.

Cracked around the edges.

No autotune. No filters.

Just *him.*

"They call it survival,
but nobody talks 'bout the ache.
About how we carry the good ones
and it's our hearts that break.
They say we strong—
nah.
We just too tired to cry.
I still see light in his eyes
every time I close mine."

Brent didn't breathe.

"You saved me once,
and you never knew.
Now I'm sending this back,

'cause I'd trade every bar
just to give him to you."

The track ended.

Just wind in the background.

No outro.

No hook.

Just **truth.**

———— ❀ ————

Brent stared at the screen.

Then up at the sky.

Didn't speak.

Didn't wipe his face.

But the tears came anyway.

Not hard.

Not fast.

Just slow.

And real.

Like a man finally breaking open in the only way left to him.

The screen dimmed, but Brent didn't touch it.

Didn't replay the verse.

Didn't save it.

Didn't delete it.

Just sat.

On that step.

While the wind shifted through the trees and the porch light buzzed like it was trying to fill the silence.

A car passed down the block—slow.
Someone's dog barked once, then stopped.
The world kept moving.

But Brent?

He stayed still.

Elbows on his knees.

Head bowed.

The words still ringing in his chest like church bells after service.

"You saved me once… and you never knew."

He thought of the rooftop.

He thought of Uzi's smile.

He thought of the moment his world ended, and a voice that wasn't his son's speaking the kind of grief that *sounded like it had lived inside him for years.*

He didn't know what to do with that.

Not yet.

Didn't know how to respond.

Didn't know if he even could.

So he just sat.

Let the weight press down.

Let the truth breathe.

And for once—

didn't run from either.

Brent sat there,

on the porch where his son once laughed,
with a phone still glowing beside him,
and a voice not his own
echoing everything he couldn't say.

Not moving.

Not speaking.

Just **holding the weight.**

Because some pain you don't fix.

You **feel** it.

And you don't let go—

You learn how to carry it.

The Room That Still Breathes

A butterfly lands once—and the air never feels quite the same again. Even after it's gone, you can still feel where it was.

L ena hadn't left the room in two days.

She slept curled on his bed—if you could call it sleep. Her body rested, but her mind stayed wide open, caught somewhere between memory and prayer.

She used Uzi's hoodie as a pillow.

Still smelled like him.

Like detergent and old notebook paper. Like late nights and good dreams. Like seventeen.

The window was cracked just enough to let in a breeze.

It moved the curtains gently.

Moved the air gently.

It made the room feel like it was **still breathing.**

That's why she hadn't closed it.

That's why she hadn't moved at all.

———— 🦋 ————

The world outside had carried on.

Distant lawn mowers. A kid's laughter across the block. A bird that wouldn't stop tapping the window in the morning like it had a message and didn't care how long it took to deliver it.

Lena ignored it all.

She just kept her hand on his blanket.

Kneading it softly. The way she used to rub his back when he was a baby and couldn't sleep.

Her lips moved every now and then.

But she wasn't talking.

Not really.

Just whispering little pieces of him to herself.

Like:

"He had that freckle behind his left ear…"

"He hated peas. Always hated peas."

"He called that song 'his comic book anthem.' Said it felt like drawing in his chest."

She repeated those things not to remember.

But to **not forget.**

———— ❀ ————

A knock came at the door, soft.

Brent.

"Lena… you want anything?"

No response.

Just the breeze.

And her thumb, still circling the same spot on the blanket.

———— ❀ ————

He stood there for a while.

Mug in one hand.

Other braced against the doorframe.

The hallway light cast a soft shadow across his feet.

It was too early to be called morning.
Too late to pretend it was still night.

The house had no hours anymore.

Just pockets of time.

Before.

After.

Now.

———— 🦋 ————

He hadn't slept more than two hours the night before.

Laid in bed with his eyes open, counting the breaths between sirens in the distance and wondering which ones were headed for someone else's story.

The coffee he held had long gone cold.

He hadn't even meant to bring it to her.

It was just what he always did.

Made two cups.

One for him.

One for her.

——— 🦋 ———

He knocked again.

Softer this time.

"You should eat something, babe."

Still nothing.

Just the sound of the breeze through the cracked window.

And somewhere inside—

her grief, breathing.

——— 🦋 ———

He set the mug on the floor outside the door.

Didn't force it.

Didn't speak again.

Just rested his palm on the wood one last time before stepping away.

The wood was warm.

That's what hurt the most.

——— 🦋 ———

He walked back to the kitchen, each step slower than the last.

The mug in his hand clinked against the counter as he set it down—louder than it should have been.

He stared at it like it had done something wrong.

Then pushed it aside.

Not hard.

Just enough to say *I'm still here.*

———— 🦋 ————

He opened the fridge.

Not because he was hungry.

Just because it was a motion that used to mean something.

Orange juice.

Leftover rice.

A note Uzi had stuck to the milk carton a week ago:

"Don't drink this. It's sus."
–Uzi

Brent read it twice.

Then closed the door.

Didn't touch it.

Didn't throw it away.

Didn't even smile.

———— 🦋 ————

The mail sat in a neat stack on the counter.

He hadn't opened it in days.

But his hands moved toward it like they were on autopilot—muscle memory from a version of life that had made sense.

He flipped through:

Gas bill.

Junk ad.

A white envelope from the school.

He froze.

No logo.

Just typed letters:

"To the family of Uziel Brooks."

He didn't open it.

He couldn't.

Not yet.

He placed it on the table and slid it away like it was still hot.

———— 🦋 ————

Then the creak of a floorboard behind him.

Soft.

He turned.

His daughter stood in the doorway.

One sock on.

One off.

Hair a mess. Eyes quiet.

She didn't say anything.

Just walked over and hugged his leg.

Brent dropped to one knee.

Held her tighter than he meant to.

And whispered,

"I miss him too."

———— 🦋 ————

She didn't let go right away.

Just stood there, arms around Brent's neck, face buried in his shoulder like she was trying to disappear into him.

When she finally pulled back, she didn't say "I'm okay."

She said:

"Do you think he's still around?"

Her voice was soft.

Like a question she'd asked herself too many times before saying it out loud.

Brent looked at her—really looked.

There were traces of Uzi in her eyes.

The shape of the nose.
The tilt of the mouth.
But something else too.

That same warmth.

That same quiet hope.

He didn't have a perfect answer.

But he gave her what he had.

"I think love stays," he said. "Even when people don't."

She nodded.

Thought about it.

Then said:

"Sometimes I still feel like I'm playing with him. In my room. Like when I'm not looking straight at anything. He's just… there."

Brent swallowed hard.

"That sounds like him."

She gave him the faintest smile.

The kind that lasted exactly one second.

Then she walked to the table.

Picked up the sketchpad Uzi had left behind.

She turned a few pages.

Stopped at a blank one.

And said:

"I think I wanna draw him today."

The light outside had dimmed into that soft, purplish dusk.

Uziel's room had grown darker too—but Lena hadn't turned on the light.

She didn't need it.

She knew every shape.

Every corner.

Every scar on the desk, every worn edge on the baseboard from his restless teenage feet.

She could feel him here.

Not in a ghostly way.

Just… in the stillness.

Like the room had absorbed his rhythm and wasn't ready to let it go yet.

She'd spent hours on his bed.

Hours holding his hoodie.
Hours whispering his name.

But now she sat at his desk.
Hands resting gently on the surface.
Like she didn't want to disturb anything.

She looked at the sketchbook.

Didn't open it.

Just… *listened.*

Listened to the faint rustling of a curtain.

The creak of the fan chain.

Her own breathing.

"You were so full of life," she whispered.
"And now this room is trying so hard to remember how to hold you."

She didn't cry this time.

Just rested her fingers on the desk drawer.

Waited.

And then slowly, quietly,

she pulled it open.

The drawer didn't slide smoothly.

It stuck halfway, like it wasn't sure it wanted to give up what it was holding.

She pulled gently.

It gave.

Inside: loose pens, a broken ruler, crumpled homework.
A corner of a folded paper poked out from beneath a sheet of sketchpad stock.

She reached in.

Pulled it free.

It was a drawing—unfinished, like most of his.

Drawn in pencil with light, purposeful lines.

It was a family portrait.

Stylized, like something out of a comic book.

Each of them slightly exaggerated—Brent with broad shoulders and a stoic look, her with long flowing hair like wind, their daughter in a cape and high-tops, arms outstretched mid-flight.

And Uzi himself?

He wasn't in front.

He wasn't in the center.

He was in the *background.*

Behind them all.

Hands resting gently on each of their shoulders.

Smiling.

Wide.

The way he did when he was *most proud.*

Lena stared at it for a long time.

Her fingers moved across the page like she could feel him through the lines.

Then, as she unfolded the sketchbook page completely—

A photo slipped out.

Old.

Slightly creased.

One of the ones she thought had been lost.

Uzi at maybe age eight.

Gap-toothed.

Wearing a crooked Spider-Man mask on his head, like a crown he refused to straighten.

She had taken it during a backyard BBQ.

He'd just told a joke no one understood but laughed at anyway.

His joy was the only punchline that mattered.

———— 🦋 ————

She held both in her lap.

Drawing and photo.

Grief and memory.

And for the first time in days—

She closed her eyes…

…and smiled.

Not because it hurt less.

But because **he was still here.**

———— 🦋 ————

Lena sat there, in the quiet of his room,
with the drawing in her lap
and the photo pressed to her chest.

She didn't speak.

She didn't move.

She just let the ache shift into something softer—
something not quite healing,
but **less sharp.**

Outside, the wind stirred the curtains.

And somewhere in the hush between night and memory,

she whispered—

"I see you."

And this time, she meant it.

The Weight of What We Carry

A butterfly doesn't return to where it first took flight. But the
air always remembers the shape of its wings.

A.V. sat in the booth, headphones around his neck, but the
mic was off.

Had been for over an hour.

The beat played on loop through the studio monitors—soft, haunting,
all low-end and space.

Jace was on the other side of the glass, half-asleep in the engineer's
chair, tapping something aimlessly on his phone.

They were supposed to be recording tonight.

Finishing a track that was already halfway done.

It was meant to be a single.

But A.V. hadn't said a word into the mic.

Not since he'd sent that voice message.

Not since **Uziel's name** burned a hole in his mind and refused to fade.

———— 🦋 ————

He scrolled through the messages on his phone again.
No reply from Brent.
Not that he expected one.
He hadn't sent it for a reply.

But still.

A part of him hoped.

Maybe not for words.

But for… acknowledgment.

Some flicker of understanding.

———— 🦋 ————

He picked up his pen.
Then put it back down.

Tried again.

Wrote:

"Sometimes I feel like I'm making noise instead of music."

Stopped.

Crossed it out.

Started over.

"I didn't pull the trigger. But I left the safety off."

He stared at that one.

Let it sit.

Didn't cross it out.

———— 🦋 ————

On the wall across the studio, a photo hung of his first show.

Local spot. Cramped stage. Blurry lighting.

But in the shot—he was lit up.

Eyes closed.

Arms wide.

Like he believed in something.

He didn't know if he believed anymore.

But he knew he couldn't stay silent.

Not now.

———— 🦋 ————

He sat back down.

The pen felt different now.

Not like a weapon.

Not like a spotlight.

Just… honest.

He pulled a sheet from the notebook. No scratch-outs this time.
No rhymes.
Just a letter.

To the family of Uziel Brooks,

You don't know me by name.

But I know your son.

Not personally.
Not with stories or sleepovers or history.
But with presence.

I felt him before I ever saw his face.

The way people spoke his name.

The way he smiled in that photo like he was holding the sun in his
chest and daring the world to take it from him.

I heard what happened.

And I can't make sense of it.

I've written a thousand verses, stood in front of crowds, made rooms chant my words—

But I can't write anything that explains what's been taken from you.

So instead, I wrote **something for him.**

A track.

It's not about guilt.
It's not about me.
It's just a sound I made when I sat in silence and thought about your boy.
The light he was.
The weight he still carries in this world.

I won't release it unless you say it's okay.

It's his name I want remembered.

His voice in the story—not mine.

Whatever you choose, I'll respect it.

But if there's any part of this that feels right,
I'd be honored to share it in his name.

With love and reverence,

Avery

He folded the page.

Taped it to a USB drive.

The track inside wasn't long.

Just a single verse.

No chorus.

No hook.

Just a beat and a voice.

A boy speaking to a boy he never met,
saying: I see you. I carry you. I will not let them forget.

———— 🦋 ————

The envelope came in the afternoon.

No return address.

No stamp—just dropped off by hand.

Lena had set it on the table with the rest of the mail.

She didn't ask about it.

Didn't press him to open it.

Just placed it there and said,

"I think this one's for you."

Brent sat at the kitchen table for twenty minutes before touching it.

No coffee in front of him.

No pen in his hand.

Just the envelope.

He recognized the handwriting.

Didn't know it.
But recognized it.

Something about the way the letters curved—like whoever wrote them was trying not to take up too much space.

He opened it slow.

Pulled out the letter.

Read the first line.

Stopped.

Stared at the words:
"You don't know me by name. But I know your son."

And everything in him tightened.

He read it all the way through.

No skips.

No flinches.

And when he got to the part about the track—

He looked at the USB taped to the bottom of the page like it was something fragile.

Like it might break if he held it wrong.

Like it might **hurt less** than everything else.

———— 🦋 ————

He stood.

Walked over to the laptop in the corner.

Booted it up.

Didn't plug in headphones.

Didn't wait for Lena.

Just inserted the drive.

And pressed play.

———— 🦋 ————

I never knew your son, but I heard him in the wind,
In the way the city quiets when a good one leaves again.

They said he drew heroes—what he didn't know was this:
He was already one, just hidden in a kid.

Ain't no hook in this song, just breath I needed to give,

'Cause if he still walked these streets, we'd all remember
how to live.
Some lights don't last long—but they don't have to,
They leave warmth in the dark where the sky can't catch you.

I used to write to survive. I used to rhyme to escape.
But now I'm writing for the names that never got their fate.

You saved me once, and I never said your name.
Now I'm offering this back, not to clear my shame—But to say your
son was love, and I heard him from afar,

And I swear on every verse, he's brighter than my stars.

So this ain't mine to keep. It belongs to your sky.
Let the world hear his name when my voice starts to rise.

Rest easy, young king.
We won't forget the shine.
Your shadow's still moving.
Your fire's still mine."

When it ended, the room went still.

No outro. No credits. Just the quiet after a storm that never raised its voice.

Brent sat at the kitchen table…

Hands clenched.

Eyes full.

Breath stuck halfway between breaking and **beginning again.**

———— 🦋 ————

Lena was folding laundry in Uziel's room.

Not because it needed to be done.

Not because she wanted to.

But because her hands didn't know what else to do.

She moved quietly—folded one of his hoodies, paused, pressed it to her face, then placed it back in the drawer she still hadn't had the strength to close.

She heard the track before she saw him.

Soft.

From the hallway.

No beat at first—just words. Clear. Steady. Real.

She froze.

Turned her head.

Brent stood at the doorway.

No expression.

Just **holding the laptop** like it weighed more than his body.

"You need to hear this," he said.

She didn't ask what it was.

Didn't ask who it was.

She followed him back to the kitchen in silence.

He hit play.

And they listened.

Together.

———— 🦋 ————

This time, she didn't cry.

Not until the final line.

"Your fire's still mine."

Her hands went to her chest.

She didn't sob.

She just broke—quietly, beautifully—like a glass vase tipping in slow motion.

And Brent?

He didn't touch her.

Not yet.

He just let the track **do its work**.

Because some things don't need comfort.

Some things just need to be **witnessed.**

The track ended.

Silence returned like a blanket.

Not the kind that comforts.

The kind that reminds you **how much space one voice can take up when it's gone.**

Lena wiped her face with the sleeve of Uzi's sweatshirt.

She stared at the laptop for a long time, then said—

"It felt like… he was talking *to* him."

Brent nodded, jaw clenched.
His hands were still locked around the edge of the table.

"I know."

He didn't say *it helped.*

Didn't say *it hurt* either.

Just:

"I think he meant it."

Lena glanced at him.

Eyes red. Tired.

But clear.

"You think people should hear it?"

Brent didn't answer right away.

Just looked out the window—
the same one Uzi used to run past every afternoon
coming home from school.

"Yeah," he said, eventually.
"I think… it's what he would've wanted."

Lena nodded.

"Then we tell him yes."

She didn't smile.

But something in her posture softened.

Like she was finally letting go of *one thing*—

so, she could hold onto something else.

Something Worth
Leaving Behind

*A butterfly doesn't announce itself. It just moves—and lets
the world feel what comes after.*

————  ————

A .V. sat on the edge of his bed.

The sun was just starting to break over the skyline, slicing the
city into warm gold and long shadows.

He hadn't slept.

Didn't want to.

Not before this.

The track was loaded.
The artwork simple—just a drawing of a crown sketched in Uzi's
style, taken from one of the images Lena had shared.
The caption was already typed:

"For Uziel Brooks.
Rest easy, young king.
Shared with permission from the family.
#SunshineStillShines"

He hovered over the "Post" button for a long second.

His thumb was trembling.

Then—

He pressed it.

And let it go.

———— 🦋 ————

No blast.
No announcement.
Just a verse.
Released into a world that didn't deserve it, but needed it anyway.

———— 🦋 ————

Later that morning, Brent sat at the kitchen table with a mug of coffee he hadn't touched.

He didn't know why he kept making it.

Habit, maybe.

Lena entered quietly, still in Uzi's hoodie, her hands wrapped around the sleeves like she didn't trust them to stay still.

She didn't speak.

Just turned her phone toward him.

A.V.'s post was up.

Already climbing.

5,642 shares.
2,800 comments.
Countless candles in the comment section.
Praying hands.
Spider-Man emojis.
Gold hearts.

But no noise.

No sensationalism.

Just **love.**

———— 🦋 ————

Brent tapped the post.

The track began to play.

Again.

But this time, it echoed different.

Not just in the house.

But in the *world.*

The track played through the city like a prayer someone had finally said out loud.

No billboards.

No promo run.

Just *word of mouth.*

And **everyone listening**.

In the school hallway, one of Uzi's classmates pulled his earbuds out halfway through the track.
Not because he didn't want to hear it.

Because he didn't know how to handle the way it made his chest feel.

His friends didn't talk about it.

They just passed the phone around, one by one,
and nodded when it reached them.

In a corner barbershop, the youngest apprentice stopped sweeping halfway through the verse and whispered,

"That's Uzi, ain't it?"

Mr. Ray nodded once.

Didn't speak.

Just turned the volume up.

———— 🦋 ————

At the park, someone had brought a portable speaker.
Set it next to the mural wall.
No announcement. No crowd.
Just music.

And slowly—people came.

Not to dance.
Not to party.

Just to stand.

To listen.

To remember.

———— 🦋 ————

In a middle school art room, a substitute teacher pressed play on the
classroom speakers while students colored in silence.

At the end, one of the kids said:

"That didn't feel like a song."

"It felt like... somebody *knew* him."

At Tony's Diner, the waitress didn't say a word when it came on through a customer's phone.

She just grabbed a Sharpie.

Walked to the Specials board.

And wrote:
"Sunshine Still Shines."

Underlined it twice.

And at the curb where **it** happened—

someone placed a small Bluetooth speaker in the grass, next to a candle and a cracked Spider-Man figure.

The track played on loop.

All night.

No one touched it.

He sat on the edge of his bed, phone in hand.

The track had only been up for hours, but his notifications were flooded.
He'd turned them off.

Didn't need the noise.
He wasn't chasing numbers.

He was **watching faces.**

Comments.
Captions.
Clips.

A boy holding back tears on his bus ride to school, whispering along with the verse.

A teacher lighting a candle at the front of her classroom.

A stranger tagging him in a video of the curb, lit by candles, the mural wall in the background.

"Didn't know him. But I feel him.
This one changed me. Thank you."

———— 🦋 ————

A.V. locked the screen.

Held the phone to his chest.

Leaned back into the bed and stared at the ceiling.

There was no joy in this.

Just... clarity.

The clearest he'd felt in years.

This wasn't his story anymore.

It never was.

It was **Uzi's**.

It was **Brent's**.

It was every kid who thought kindness wasn't armor,
every parent who believed love could protect them,
every artist who wondered if their voice could **matter**.

He whispered, barely loud enough for the room to hear—

"Let them have it."

And for once,

he didn't mean the applause.

He meant **the light**.

————— ❦ —————

Brent stood by the window, arms crossed.

He'd been watching the street for a while now.

Nothing special.
Just cars passing.
A jogger with headphones.
A kid on a skateboard—too young to know what had been lost here,
but maybe old enough to feel it.

He saw the chalk again.

The words on the sidewalk in front of the house.

"Uzi was light."
"Shine forever."

Someone had written *#SunshineStillShines* in bold, messy handwriting.

He hadn't seen who.

Didn't need to.

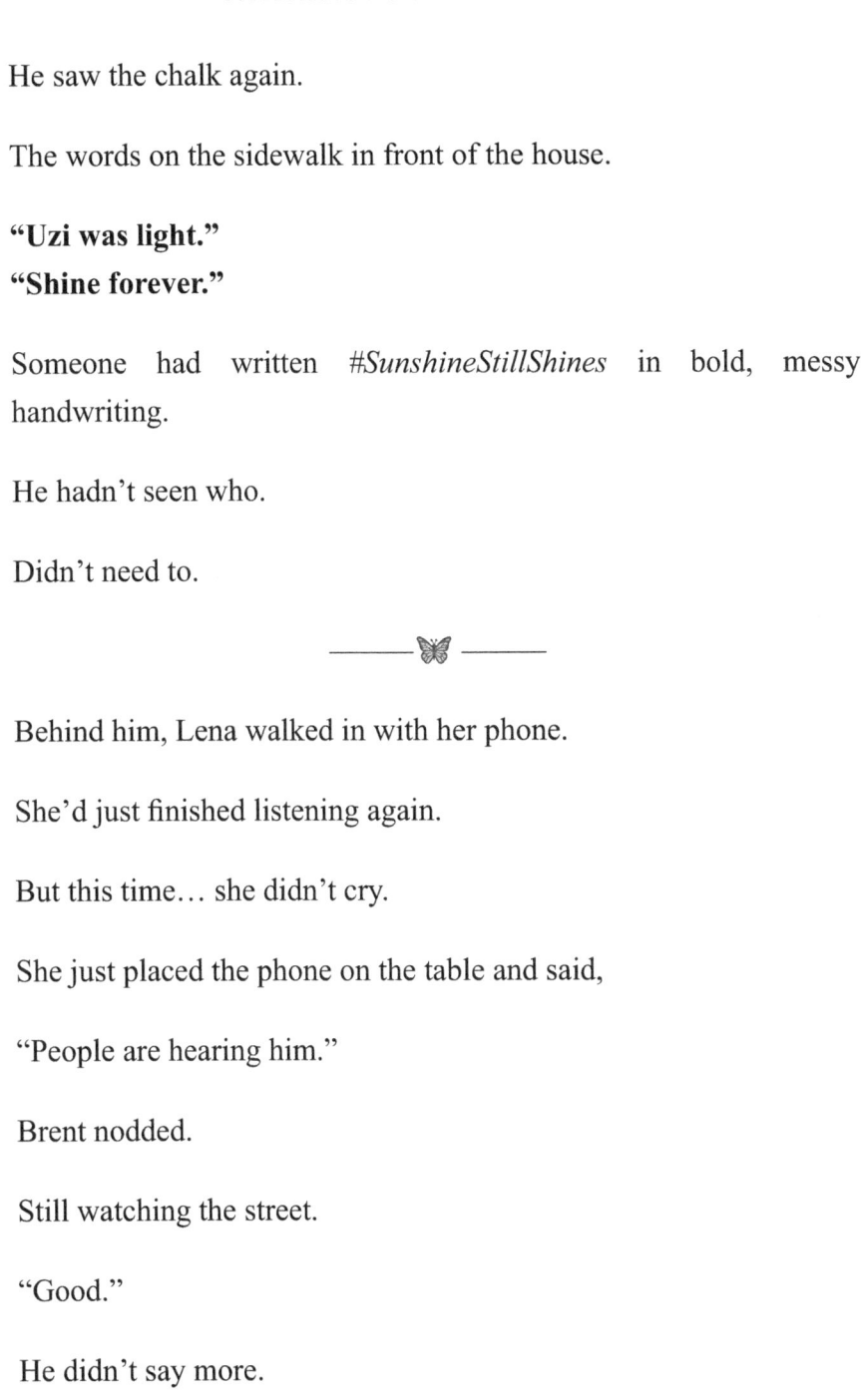

Behind him, Lena walked in with her phone.

She'd just finished listening again.

But this time… she didn't cry.

She just placed the phone on the table and said,

"People are hearing him."

Brent nodded.

Still watching the street.

"Good."

He didn't say more.

Didn't have to.

Because in the living room, their daughter had drawn something new:

A superhero—bright blue cape, bold black curls, gold heart on his chest.
Floating just above the ground, hand outstretched.

And on the edge of the drawing, written in careful, blocky letters:

"Uzi lives in the light now."

Outside, the wind picked up.
The chalk shimmered under the streetlamp.
And inside, the house held more than grief.

It held **legacy.**

What We Build from the Ashes

Some butterflies die in flight—and still leave trails of color in
the sky. Not every end is an ending. Some are beginnings in
disguise.

A.V. sat on the studio floor, back against the soundproof wall,
knees pulled in, notebook open across his lap.

He hadn't written anything new since the track.

He couldn't.

Not because the words weren't coming.

But because they *didn't feel like enough anymore.*

He stared at the pages—verses, hooks, metaphors—and they all
looked so small.
Sharp. Clever. Emotional.
But **small.**

What good were bars when kids were dying at intersections?

What good was a rhyme if it stopped at the headphones?

——— 🦋 ———

His phone buzzed again.

He didn't check it.

He already knew what it was:

Messages.
Reposts.
More people thanking him for the song.
More people saying they'd cried.

And that was good.

But it wasn't **change**.

——— 🦋 ———

His eyes drifted to the corner of the studio—where an old poster leaned against the wall.
A flyer from his first open mic.

He remembered what it felt like back then.

Scared.
Hungry.
Honest.

He didn't want to be famous.

He just wanted **to matter**.

Now he was famous.

But it still didn't feel like **enough**.

———— 🦋 ————

He flipped to a fresh page in his notebook.

Wrote:

"Music is a key, not the door."

He circled it.

Hard.

Then underlined it twice.

And below that—

he wrote something else:

"What if we built something real?"

———— 🦋 ————

He flipped the page again.

The first line came out sloppy, rushed:

"Youth center?"

He stared at it.

Didn't like the word. Too sterile.

Crossed it out.

Wrote underneath:

"A place for kids to write. Talk. Create. Feel safe."

Circled it.

Then added more:

"No judgment."
"No uniforms."
"Open late."
"Free art supplies."
"Mic nights."
"Counselors—not cops."

He sat back, eyes wide—not with excitement, but **recognition.**

This wasn't new.

This was what **he** had needed.

What **his friends** had needed.

What **Uzi** might've loved.

———— 🦋 ————

He stood up, still holding the notebook.

Started pacing the studio.

The words kept coming:

"Spoken word sessions."
"Studios. Not just recording booths—**safe booths.**"
"Workshops."
"Guest artists."
"Grief circles."

He flipped to another blank page.

Started sketching.

Not a floor plan—just a feeling.

A shape.

A space with color. Warm light.
A place that didn't feel like survival.

A place that **felt like staying.**

———— ❦ ————

He paused.

Looked down at the notes.

Then whispered to the room:

"You'd have drawn the whole wall, wouldn't you, Uzi?"

He smiled.

First time in a long while that it didn't hurt to do so.

He sat back on the stool again, notebook in his lap.

The sketches had started to take shape—rough layouts of open rooms, ideas for murals, a recording space that doubled as a therapy corner, couches instead of desks.

He could see it all.

But something was missing.

Someone.

Someone who could walk into that space and make a kid feel safe without saying a word.

Someone who could teach a different kind of strength—one that wasn't loud or hard or bulletproof.

Someone who had already saved him once, without even knowing what he was saving.

He turned to a fresh page.

Wrote at the top:

"Brent."

Just the name.

He stared at it.

Then underlined it.

Slow.

———— 🦋 ————

Could he ask?

Would Brent even want to speak to him again?

Could a father who lost his son work beside the voice that played when the world cracked open?

Maybe not.

Maybe never.

But still…

A.V. wrote:

"Not to run it. Not to lead.
Just… to *be there*.
For the kids who need someone solid."
"The way he was for me."

He stared at those words until they blurred.

Then whispered:

"You were my foundation.
Maybe you can help build theirs."

———— 🦋 ————

He turned the page.

Not for a rhyme.

Not for a chorus.

Just for **clarity.**

At the top, he wrote:

"To Brent Brooks."

Then paused.

Stared at those words like they might vanish if he blinked too long.

He hadn't said the man's name out loud in years.
Hadn't *dared* to.

But now it felt right.

Not comfortable.

Not easy.

Just... right.

———— 🦋 ————

He exhaled.

Pressed the pen to the paper again.

"You don't owe me anything.
I know that.
I don't expect a reply."

"But I've been sitting with this weight since your son's name
reached me.
Since I saw your face on that screen and realized—
I knew you long before the uniform."

"You were the first person who ever told me I mattered without asking
me to prove it first."

He stopped.
Ran his hand over his jaw.

Then kept going.

"I've been thinking...
If there had been a space—
back then—
where a kid like me could go after school…
write…
speak…
breathe without looking over his shoulder—
maybe I would've made it here without needing to almost die first."

———— ✖ ————

"I want to build that space."

"For kids like me.
For kids like yours."

"I'll pay for it. I'll run it. I'll handle everything."

"But I want to ask you something.
Not to manage it.
Not to carry it."

"Just…
Would you come sit with them?"

"The way you once sat with me?"

———— 🦋 ————

He stopped.

Set the pen down.

Read the letter twice.

No edits.

No polish.

Just **truth.**

Then he folded the page.
Slipped it into an envelope.
Wrote **"Brent"** on the front.

And sat there.

Still.

Listening to the silence like it might answer for him.

He didn't drive.

Didn't ask Malik to come with him.

Just walked.

Through blocks he hadn't touched in years,
wearing a hoodie, cap low,
heart steady but unsure.

The envelope felt heavy in his jacket pocket.
Not because of the paper—
but because of everything it *meant*.

He paused across the street from the house.

Didn't move right away.

It looked exactly like he remembered from the news clip.

Except now, the porch had two folding chairs on it.

One was empty.

The other held a pair of shoes—little ones. Uzi's sister, maybe.

There was chalk on the sidewalk.

"Uzi was light."

His chest tightened.

But he didn't turn back.

———— 🦋 ————

He walked up the steps slow.

Didn't knock.

Just stood there, letter in hand.

He thought maybe Brent would open the door.

Or Lena.

Or nobody.

He didn't know which would be harder.

So instead, he reached for the mailbox.

Slid the envelope in.

No note on the outside.

No initials.

Just:

Brent.

———— 🦋 ————

He stood there a moment longer.

Long enough to let the weight settle.

Long enough to say—without speaking—

I see you.
I'm here.
And this time… I came back.

Then he stepped off the porch.

Hands in his pockets.

Eyes on the pavement.

And walked back the way he came.

———— 🦋 ————

He didn't check the mail every day anymore.

Most of it didn't matter—bills, cards, well-meaning condolences he hadn't opened, a few hand-addressed envelopes from people who thought healing could be mailed in.

But today…
something pulled him to the door.

———— 🦋 ————

He stepped onto the porch, barefoot.
The wood was warm beneath his feet.
Sunlight draped across the steps in that soft, *late afternoon* way.

The chalk was still there—
slightly faded now, but still legible.

"Uzi was light."

He let his eyes rest on it for a second longer than usual.

Then opened the mailbox.

———— 🦋 ————

One envelope.

No return address.

No postage.

Just his name, written clean on the front.

Brent.

That was it.

No last name.
No formality.
Just Brent.

The handwriting was familiar.

But something about it…
felt *careful.*

———— 🦋 ————

He brought it inside.

Sat at the kitchen table.

Tore it open.

Unfolded the letter.

Read the first line.

"You don't owe me anything."

His eyes narrowed.

He kept reading.

Line by line.

Until he got to the part that stopped his hands mid-air:

"I want to build that space.
For kids like me.
For kids like yours."

And then:

"Would you come sit with them?
The way you once sat with me?"

———— 🦋 ————

Brent leaned back in his chair.

Set the letter down.

Stared at the ceiling.

Not because he was searching for answers—
but because he finally realized…

someone else had been searching too.

He found her in Uzi's room.

Not lying on the bed this time.

She was sitting at his desk,
running her finger along the edge of a drawing Uzi never finished.

Her back was to the door,
but she knew it was him the second he stepped in.

He didn't speak right away.

Didn't hand her the letter.

Just stood there for a moment,
watching her in the soft blue light filtering through the window.

She looked over her shoulder.

"You okay?"

He nodded.

But that wasn't the truth.

So he tried again.

"I got a letter."

She turned to face him fully now.

"From who?"

He walked across the room.

Held it out.

"A.V."

She didn't flinch.

Didn't stiffen.

Just… took it.

Like she'd expected something like this.

Like maybe a part of her had been waiting for it.

———— 🦋 ————

She read it slowly.

Line by line.

One hand at her chest.

The other holding the letter like it was glass.

When she reached the end, she looked up at him.

Eyes full.
But not broken.

"He wants to build something," she said.

Brent nodded.

"He wants me there."

Lena ran her thumb over Uzi's name in the letter.

Then whispered—

"Uzi would've loved that."

Brent sat beside her, their knees touching under the desk where Uzi once scribbled dreams in ink and graphite.

The letter lay between them,
creased now,
warmed by their hands,
heavy with possibility.

He looked at her,
voice soft.
Not fragile.
Just *real.*

"Should we do it?"

Lena didn't hesitate.

Didn't smile.

Just nodded.

Once.

"Yeah," she said.
"Let's build something he would've run to."

A Place to Land

A butterfly never sees its own wings. But still, it learns to trust the wind—and somewhere, something blooms because it did.

T he building didn't look like much.

Peeling paint.

Boarded windows.

A sagging roofline that creaked when pigeons landed on it.

It used to be a rec center.

Then a church basement.

Then nothing.

Just another forgotten space in a city full of them.

But A.V. didn't see what it was.

He saw **what it could be**.

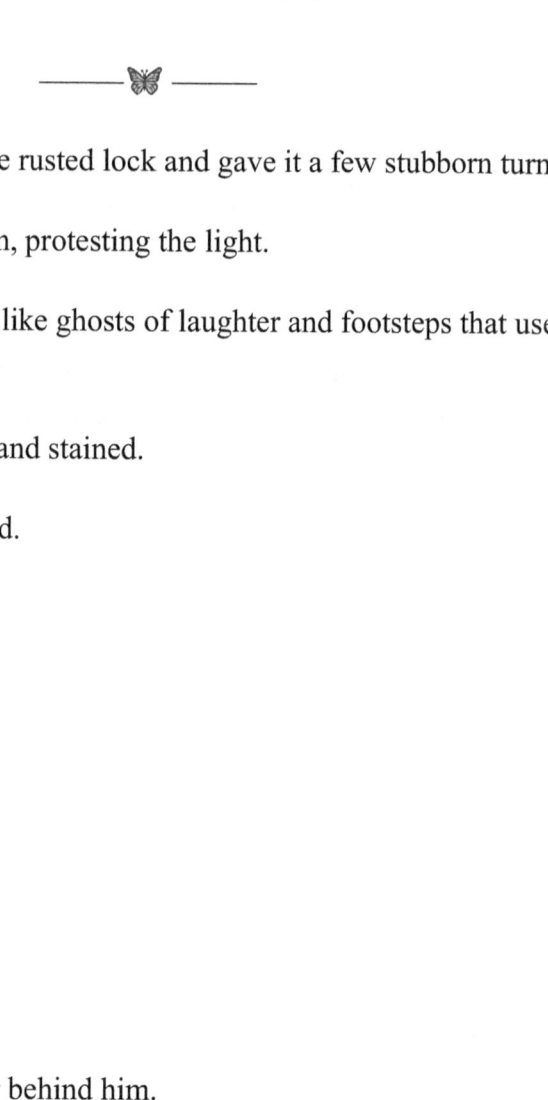

He slid the key into the rusted lock and gave it a few stubborn turns.

The door groaned open, protesting the light.

Dust danced in the air like ghosts of laughter and footsteps that used to live here.

The floor was scuffed and stained.

The walls were cracked.

But the room was big.

Wide.

Open.

He stepped inside.

Alone at first.

Then—

the sound of a car door behind him.

He turned.

Brent.

Lena.

And their daughter, standing between them, holding a sketchpad.

———— 🦋 ————

They walked in without a word.

No ceremony.

No speeches.

Just eyes scanning the space.

Lena ran her hand along the wall near the entrance.

Paint flaked off like old memories.

"It smells like dust and old basketballs," she said.

A.V. smiled, small.

"That means it's perfect."

———— 🦋 ————

Brent walked to the center of the room.

Looked up at the light coming through a crack in the ceiling.

"You really want to do this here?"

A.V. nodded.

"Yeah. I do."

Brent turned in a slow circle.

Took it in.

The damage.

The potential.

The *need.*

Then he said:

"Good bones."

———— 🦋 ————

They stood in a rough circle near the center of the room.

Light filtered through a high window, casting long shadows across the worn floor.

A.V. looked at Brent.

"This isn't a studio," he said.
"Not a hangout. Not a second-chance center.
I don't want them walking in here thinking they have to be broken to belong."

Brent nodded slowly.

"So what is it?"

A.V. didn't answer right away.

He looked down at the floor, then back up.

"It's a place to land.
Whether you're flying, falling… or just tired of holding it all in."

Lena stepped closer, running her fingers along the edge of a broken window frame.

"It needs color," she said.
"Not just on the walls. I mean… *energy.*
Light. Laughter. Movement. It can't feel like a place where trauma goes to be analyzed."

A.V. smiled.

"Exactly."

Their daughter tugged at Lena's sleeve.

"Can we paint Spider-Man on one of the walls?"

Lena looked at Brent.

Then at A.V.

And everyone just knew—

"Yeah," Lena said softly.
"I think we kind of have to."

Brent leaned against the wall.

"No cops. Not inside. Not in uniform."

A.V. nodded.

"Agreed."

"No fake positivity either," Brent added.
"If a kid's angry, let them be. Let 'em speak. Just… give them room
to get it out."

"Music. Art. Space. Community," A.V. said.
"No therapy that feels like punishment. No rules that feel
like cages."

Lena stepped forward.

Her voice firmer now.

"It needs to feel like Uzi."

Everyone went still.

That name still hurt.

Still hummed in the bones.

But no one flinched.

"It needs to feel like kindness."

After the conversation quieted,
Lena and her daughter wandered toward the far wall.

It faced the front windows.
The ones that let in the morning light.

The wall was cracked, streaked with old paint and water damage.
But it was **the one.**

You could just feel it.

Lena knelt down beside her daughter.

"You think this is it?"

The girl looked up at the wall like it was a sky waiting to be drawn on.

"Yeah. This is where he'd be."

She opened her sketchpad.

Flipped to the last page she'd been working on.

Held it up.

It was Uzi—
in comic book style.
A golden hoodie instead of a cape.
A mural brush in one hand.
A web-sling from the other.

Above him, in big letters:

"Kindness is a superpower."

Lena pressed her fingers to her lips.

Then leaned in and whispered,

"We'll paint it together."

The Haven

A butterfly doesn't know the lives it changes—only that it
was made to move. What it becomes... lives on in color.

T he building still creaked when the wind hit it just right.
Some things don't change.

But inside?
It was alive.

Walls filled with color.
Laughter echoing off wood that once held silence.
Beats thumping from the studio.
Paint splattered on shoes, jeans, floor tiles, *faces*.

This wasn't just a youth center.

This was **The Haven.**

On the back wall—the mural stood twenty feet high.

Uzi in his golden hoodie.
Brush in one hand.
Spider-Man's web spiraling from the other.
The words above him clear as ever:

"Kindness is a superpower."

Some of the new kids called him "Sunshine."

They didn't know him.
But they felt him.
And that was enough.
Because love doesn't end.
Love loves when we love.

In the corner, A.V. stood behind the mic with a kid no older than fifteen.

Nervous.

Hands shaking.

A.V. crouched beside him.

Whispered:

"You don't have to be loud to be heard.
Just be real."

The boy nodded.

Took a breath.

And stepped up.

Out in the main room, Lena was at the art table with two girls working on a mosaic.

They were giggling.
One dropped a tile.
It shattered.

"Oops."

"It's okay," Lena said, smiling.
"Even broken pieces belong somewhere."

And Brent?

He sat in the reading nook.

A group of boys gathered around him.

They weren't reading.

They were just **talking.**

About life.
About their week.
About how one of them had gotten into a fight and didn't know how to say sorry.

Brent listened.

Then said:

"Strong don't mean hard.
Strong means honest."

And they nodded.

Not because it sounded cool.

But because it felt **true.**

──── 🦋 ────

Near the mural wall, a new kid—maybe ten, maybe eleven—was running too fast, chasing someone around the chairs.

He tripped.

Landed in a burst of laughter.

"Ow," he groaned, rubbing his elbow.

One of the other kids said, "Why'd you even run like that?"

The boy sat up, grinning through the scrape.

Shrugged.

And said:

"I don't know, man.

Blame it on the butterflies."

The room laughed.

And somewhere, beneath the echo,

you could almost hear wings.

About the Author

R yan McGraw is a writer, scientist, and father of two who believes that love isn't just something we feel—it's something we do. Born in California and raised across the Midwest as a military brat, Ryan grew up learning how to adapt, observe, and quietly wonder about the why behind everything. He now lives with his loving wife and children, who keep his heart full, his house loud, and his coffee cold.

Blame It on the Butterflies is his debut novel—written as a reminder that life is short, but love can ripple forever. If this story moved you, changed you, or just made you pause for a minute, Ryan would love to hear from you.

🦋 You can reach him at: **BlameitontheButterflies@GMail.com**

Just be kind.